A Bitter S

A Chocolate Centered Cozy Mystery Series

Cindy Bell

Copyright © 2016 Cindy Bell

All rights reserved.

All rights reserved. No part of this publication may be reproduced or transmitted in any form or by any means, electronic or mechanical, including photocopy, recording, or any information storage or retrieval system, without permission in writing from the publisher.

This is a work of fiction. The characters, incidents and locations portrayed in this book and the names herein are fictitious. Any similarity to or identification with the locations, names, characters or history of any person, product or entity is entirely coincidental and unintentional.

All trademarks and brands referred to in this book are for illustrative purposes only, are the property of their respective owners and not affiliated with this publication in any way. Any trademarks are being used without permission, and the publication of the trademark is not authorized by, associated with or sponsored by the trademark owner.

ISBN-13: 978-1523809103

ISBN-10: 1523809108

Table of Contents

Chapter One 1

Chapter Two 20

Chapter Three 29

Chapter Four 44

Chapter Five 53

Chapter Six 74

Chapter Seven 95

Chapter Eight 113

Chapter Nine 128

Chapter Ten 147

Chapter Eleven 162

Chapter Twelve 184

Chapter Thirteen 195

Chapter Fourteen 203

Chapter Fifteen 215

Chapter Sixteen 229

Chocolate Cupcake Recipe 238

More Cozy Mysteries by Cindy Bell 241

Chapter One

The crinkle of the wrapper gave Ally a sense of satisfaction. She carefully wrapped up the chocolate and tied a small, thin ribbon around the top.

"You will look perfect on someone's pillow."

"Good job, Ally." Charlotte walked up with a tray full of caramel mousse chocolates.

"Thanks. Are they ready?" Ally asked as she looked at the tray.

"I'm afraid not. They took too long to set and I haven't even been able to drizzle them yet. But if you want you can take what's left from the test batch. I think there are a couple left."

"Okay. I'm sure the mint chocolates and dark truffles will be enough. That is what we agreed to bring. The caramel ones were just an afterthought, anyway. I can take them another time."

"Don't be nervous, sweetheart, you're going to

do great." Charlotte patted Ally's cheek with a soft touch. "All you have to do is show up and they are going to ask for the pen to sign the deal."

"I don't know, I spoke to Denise on the phone this morning. She said the manager wants to see what we have, and also wants to tour the shop to see where the chocolates are made." Ally chewed on her bottom lip for a moment. "That doesn't sound so simple."

"It's going to be just fine. Denise already got us in the door. With that kind of good luck you know that this is going to go well."

"I'm just glad that I'll get to see her. Until you mentioned her last week I had forgotten all about her."

"Of course you did. You were only a young girl when she and your mother were friends." Charlotte smiled sadly. "It's still hard sometimes for me to see some of her friends."

"I know, it must be." Ally caressed her grandmother's hand as the loss of Ally's mother still affected them both.

"But it is always good to have an old friend

come back. And with the hotel just opening, it's the perfect opportunity for us to link our business with theirs." Charlotte plucked one of the ribbons on a chocolate mint candy. "These look fabulous. You did a great job, Ally."

"You don't think it's too much to leave on a pillow?"

"I think it's just enough. Remember, this isn't the most traditional hotel, they want to be different, they want to mix traditional and modern. These chocolates might just help them accomplish that." Charlotte closed up the box of samples that Ally planned to take with her to the hotel. "It's not just about work either. I hope that you will take the time to enjoy yourself during your stay."

"It's only one night. But it might be nice to be away from all of the meowing and snorting."

"Oh yes, I'll be dealing with those two."

"I think they somehow know that you're staying and they're looking forward to it. Arnold's tail was wagging this morning, and Peaches has been sitting on your favorite chair."

"Trust me, the feeling is mutual. I've missed Arnold snuggling up to me at night."

"Only you would cuddle with a pot-bellied pig."

"He's very warm!"

"I bet." Ally laughed. "All right, I'm going to head out I guess. Any last minute advice for me?"

"I find it's always good to make a personal connection with people. Notice little things about the staff. Remember their names. If you do that then they are more likely to remember and recommend the chocolates."

"Good idea. I will do my best. See you tomorrow." Ally gave her grandmother a quick but firm hug. She picked up the box of chocolates and a box of chocolate cupcakes and walked towards the door.

On her way to the door Charlotte called out to her. "Don't forget to bring me some of those cute little shampoos!"

Ally laughed as she started to push open the door. She was too distracted to notice that someone had already opened it from the other side. When she turned to lean against the door, she pushed into Luke's broad chest instead.

"Easy there." He grinned and caught her arm to steady her. The moment he touched her, she became flustered.

"Sorry, I didn't see you there."

"It's okay." He smiled and held the door open for her. "Where are you off to?"

"I get to spend the night at the new hotel that opened up in Mainbry."

"Oh? For business?"

"Yes. I'm going to try to woo them with my chocolates."

"I see." He reached into the box of chocolates and tried to grab one.

"Hands off the merchandise, mister." She quirked a brow as she moved the box away from him.

"Aw." He stuck out his bottom lip and winked at her.

"How can I resist that look?" Ally knew that he wasn't a fan of dark chocolate so she picked a mint chocolate out of the box and handed it to him. "Now, you can't eat that right this second."

"No? Why not?"

"It's supposed to go on your pillow."

"Hm. So I'll dream of you?"

"Ha ha." Ally rolled her eyes and looked away before he could see the blush that rose in her cheeks. "Or maybe, so you have a treat before you crawl into bed."

"I've never understood the chocolate on your pillow thing. When are you supposed to brush your teeth? Do you eat the candy first? Do you brush and then eat the candy and then brush again?" Luke shook his head. "That's why I don't stay in fancy places."

"You're funny, Luke." Ally grinned at him. "I'm sure that you have not spent that much time thinking about chocolates on pillows."

"This one, I will put on my pillow. I will make sure that it is there tonight before I go to sleep. Because it's from you."

"Thanks Luke." Ally blushed. "Do you want to walk me to my car?"

"Sure." As they approached the car Ally

glanced back at the shop to see her grandmother peeking out through the large window at the front of the shop. As soon as Charlotte discovered she was caught, she ducked out of the window. Ally smiled to herself. Her grandmother did enjoy playing matchmaker.

"Let me get that for you." Luke opened the passenger door for her. Ally set the box of samples and cupcakes inside.

"Thank you, Luke. I'm sorry, I didn't even ask you why you were stopping by."

"I just wanted to check in, see how everything's going. I know it's been a while since we've seen each other."

"Over a week." She met his eyes as she closed the door. "I was beginning to think that you had forgotten about me."

Luke rested one hand on the top of the car beside where she stood.

"I could never forget you, Ally, not for a second."

"I'm not sure if that's a good thing or a bad thing." She laughed. He looked into her eyes as her laughter faded into a nervous giggle.

"I think it is a good thing." He stood up from the car and walked around the front to open the driver's side door for her. "Have a safe trip, okay?"

"I will." She smiled and got into the car. It was difficult to drive away from him. She had the sense that he wanted to say more, or maybe he wanted her to say more, but she still believed that many things were better left unsaid.

***

The drive to Mainbry wasn't very long, but Ally savored it. She rolled down the windows and let the wind blow through her hair. With the radio cranked up she sang along to one of her favorite songs. She had a lot to feel positive about. As the manager of the chocolate shop she had taken on a lot of responsibility, but she found that she enjoyed it. The important thing was that her grandmother now had more freedom to enjoy her time, which she was, in the senior community of Freely Lakes.

When Ally pulled into the parking lot of the hotel she was a little surprised. The hotel was a bit smaller than she expected, and it was also blue. From top to bottom it was blue. It occurred to her that the hotel might have fit in better in Blue River than in Mainbry. She drove through the canopied entrance and found a parking valet waiting for her. He stepped out and opened the door for her.

"Is there anywhere I can just park it?" Ally asked.

"Don't worry I'll take good care of it."

"All right, let me just get my things." Ally grabbed her overnight bag and the boxes of sample chocolates and cupcakes.

"Name please."

"Ally Sweet." He wrote down her name on a slip of paper.

"I'll get that taken up to your room," he said as he gestured to the overnight bag.

"Thanks." She smiled and handed over her bag and car keys to the valet.

"No problem. I'll be careful, I promise." The valet held up the car keys.

Ally laughed as he drove her car away from the hotel entrance. She took a moment to smooth down her hair as the wind had tousled the brown tresses. Once she felt that she looked her best she started towards the door. Before she could reach it, someone walked right in front of her. She took a step back to avoid walking into him.

"Excuse me, I'm sorry." He turned to face her. His light brown eyes met hers as he offered a sheepish smile. "Head of security, and I didn't even see you there."

"It's okay." Ally smiled and offered him her hand. "I'm Ally Sweet."

"Dustin Keeris." He shook her hand and smiled at her. "It's nice to meet you. Are you staying here?"

"Just for the night. I'm here to pitch my chocolates for the turndown service. Would you like to try one?" She started to open the box.

"What kind are they?" He smiled.

"We have a choice of milk mint chocolates or dark chocolate truffles."

"Oh, no thanks. I really don't like mint or dark chocolate, it's too bitter. But it was nice of you to offer. Are you meeting with Denise?"

"Yes."

"I can take you to her. Just give me one second. I just have to drop this master key off at the front desk." Ally waited as he gave the key to the lady behind the desk. He was a slender man, a little taller than average. He looked to be in his fifties. Ally watched as the lady behind the desk placed it behind the counter. Dustin walked back to her. "Follow me." Dustin led her through the lobby and down a side hallway. He paused in front of a door that had a sign on it and knocked twice. "Denise? You in there?"

The door swung open and Denise stepped out. Ally recognized her right away from her bright red curls. Ally remembered winding them around her fingers and even tugging on them now and then as a young child.

"Denise, it's good to see you."

"Oh wow, Ally! Let me look at you." She took a step back and looked her over from head to toe. "It's uncanny." Her eyes widened. "You look just like your mother."

"Oh, thank you." Ally smiled. "You don't look

any different than I remember."

"Now, that I find hard to believe." Denise grinned. "Did you meet Dustin?"

"Yes. Thanks for your help, Dustin," Ally said.

"No problem. I'm staying here tonight to test out some new security measures I put in place. If you need anything, Denise." He met her eyes.

"Thanks Dustin." She smiled as he walked away. Then she turned back to Ally. "So, what did you bring me?"

"First things first, these are from Mee-Maw." She displayed the box of chocolate cupcakes.

"Oh yes, my favorite! I love her so much!" Denise took the box and grinned. "I suppose I'm going to have to find someone to share these with."

"Hey, I won't tell." Ally winked.

"Good."

"Now, down to business, I hope you'll like what I've brought for you to sample."

"I'm sure I will."

"These are the chocolates that will go on the pillows." Ally pointed to the chocolates. "These are the dark truffles and these are the mint chocolates? Would you like to try one?"

"Yes." She plucked one out and unwrapped it. "Nice packaging."

Ally smiled. Denise popped the mint chocolate in her mouth and nodded.

"Just as I expected, absolutely delicious. Too bad I really do have to share these. Just a second." She waved to a woman who walked down the hall.

"Lisa, remember I told you we're going to try a chocolate with our turndown service?"

"Yes ma'am." The young woman paused beside her.

"This is Ally. Ally, this is Lisa, she's in charge of turndown. You can leave the chocolates with her, and then enjoy the rest of your time at the hotel." Her phone buzzed. She frowned as she looked at a text. "Because I have to get going. A crisis in the kitchen. Sorry Ally."

"It's okay, I understand. I'm sure I'll be in good hands with Lisa."

Lisa smiled at her. Denise grabbed a dark truffle and walked away. Ally showed Lisa the chocolates. "These are the mint chocolates and dark truffles to go on the pillows. Put one of each in every room that is occupied. You're welcome to try them as there should be more than enough."

"What are these?" Lisa pointed to the two caramel chocolates.

"Oh, I forgot about those. I have an idea. If you don't mind, could you make sure that Dustin Keeris gets them in his room? He doesn't like mint or dark chocolate."

"Sure, no problem, I know which room he's in. Everyone does. It's like having the FBI spend the night." She grinned.

"Oh?" Ally raised an eyebrow.

"He's spending the night to make sure that we don't deviate from his security rules. It's a good thing, don't get me wrong, but it's still hard to be watched all the time."

"Yes, I'm sure it is. But by tomorrow it will be over."

"Very true." Lisa nodded. "I'll make sure these get on every pillow."

"Thanks." Ally turned back down the hall to

get her room key then she went to explore a little. The hotel did a good job of being a cross between a hotel and a quaint bed and breakfast. It had the amenities of a hotel, but the intimacy of a bed and breakfast. Ally was sure she was going to enjoy herself. She spotted a bar, a small café, and a spa right in the building. The hotel rooms appeared to be mostly on the second and third floors, while the ground floor had several conference rooms, and even a small gym. It certainly looked like the best hotel in Mainbry.

After checking out the grounds she decided to get a quick bite to eat at the café. She was hungry and finished the burger and chips quickly.

After she had finished she headed back inside to find her room. It was on the second floor towards the end of the corridor. She used the key to enter. Just as she expected, the room was as well decorated as the rest of the hotel. The bed was piled with thick blankets and plush pillows. It called to her after such a busy day. Her overnight bag was in the room. She changed into her pajamas and crawled into bed.

As she lay in bed she closed her eyes. Instantly she thought of Luke. It was something that had been happening lately. She would just be washing the dishes, or walking Arnold, and Luke would cross her mind. Only he never really left it. She decided to give him a quick call to see how his night was going. When the line went straight to voicemail she chose not to leave a message and felt a little silly for calling at all.

Luke was from the city and had no connections in town and Ally was still trying to find her feet since moving back to Blue River. They enjoyed each other's company and had become good friends. And although they flirted, she made sure it didn't go further. It wasn't that long ago that she was signing divorce papers. The idea of dating was enough to make her throat go dry. She never thought she would have to do that again. Marriage was supposed to be it. It was supposed to be forever. However, she did enjoy the flirtation that had developed between them. She was about to fall asleep when her phone rang. She picked it up, assuming it was her grandmother calling to say goodnight.

"Hello?"

"Sorry I missed your call."

Her eyes flew open. "Oh Luke, it's okay."

"Did you need something?"

She felt ridiculous for calling in the first place. What was she thinking? He had enough on his plate. He was probably working on a case.

"I just thought I'd check in on you."

"I appreciate that. Though I suspect you might be psychic, as I was just thinking about calling you. I didn't want to interrupt your evening though."

"Luke, you could never interrupt my evening. I'm happy to hear from you. How was the rest of your day?"

"It was okay. Spent most of it meeting new colleagues. We have a couple of new recruits and a new homicide detective. Apparently one detective isn't enough and nobody seems to stay put in Blue River."

"Why do you think that is?"

"I don't know. I think a lot of people just want

to be where the action is."

"There's plenty of action in Blue River."

"It sure seems that way sometimes. Hey listen, I know it's late. I don't want to keep you up, but I just wanted to check if you want to meet for breakfast tomorrow after you check out?"

Ally's eyes widened. She hadn't expected that. "Uh, sure. That would be nice."

"Great. Say, Sandy's at nine?"

"Perfect." Ally swallowed hard.

"I'm looking forward to it. Sleep well."

"I plan to." She yawned. "Good night, Luke."

"Good night, Ally."

She hung up the phone with the intention of going right to sleep. However, a few minutes later she was faced with a daunting reality. Luke wanted to meet her for breakfast in the morning. She had said yes. Breakfast was breakfast, she could handle that, but where would it lead next. What if he wanted to talk about the two of them dating? He'd dropped plenty of hints about the fact that he was interested. What if tomorrow he intended to ask her to go on a date? To make their relationship officially more than just a friendship? The thought kept her awake for some time. After thinking it through she came to the conclusion that accepting his offer was a mistake. It was too late to call so she decided to send him a text.

Luke, thanks for the invitation but I forgot I am going to try to meet with the manager of the hotel in the morning. Raincheck?

She didn't expect a reply. It was already late. Surely by now he was sound asleep. After some time Ally finally managed to drop off to sleep.

Chapter Two

When Ally woke the next morning she felt refreshed. She stretched and yawned. There was no cat parading around her pillow to get her attention. There was no pig squealing at the foot of her bed or the door to her room. She didn't have to jump up and fill their bowls. It wasn't that she didn't miss them, but being able to snuggle back into her pillow for a little longer was very nice.

She wanted to lie there longer, but she wanted enough time to speak to the manager. She shook her head and climbed out of bed.

"This is a business trip, Ally, remember?" She smiled at herself in the bathroom mirror. Her hair was ruffled from sleep. She ruffled it even more and stuck out her tongue at her reflection. Then she changed out of her pajamas and had a shower. She used her own shampoo so she could take the one from the hotel back for her grandmother. After getting ready she gathered her things. As she turned to leave the room she took one last look around to make sure that she wasn't forgetting anything. Then she snapped a picture of the room to show her grandmother. The warm colors and high windows really gave the room a glow.

Ally headed out of the room and down the hallway to check out at the front desk. As she walked she hoped that she would run into Denise again. She enjoyed the woman's company. She wondered if Dustin liked his caramel mousse chocolates. When she reached the front desk there was only a young woman behind the counter. No sign of Denise, or Dustin.

"I'd like to check out, please." Ally set her room key down on the counter.

"Thank you, I hope you enjoyed your stay." The woman smiled cheerfully at her.

"Actually, I really did. This is a very nice hotel."

"Thanks. The boss likes all of the staff to be involved and even allows some personal touches. He wants to make it feel more like a family atmosphere."

"I didn't get a chance to meet him. Is he here now?"

"No, Ben is out for the morning, but he did ask me to remind you that he wants to come out on Tuesday to look at the shop and see where the chocolates are made."

"Great. I'm looking forward to it. Thanks again."

The woman smiled and nodded to Ally as she headed for the exit. She was a little disappointed that she didn't get to speak to the manager as she would have liked a definite yes or no on the deal, but she knew she would be seeing him at the shop. She stepped out onto the front sidewalk. The valet walked up to her.

"I need my car, please. It's registered under Sweet."

"Sure thing. Give me two minutes." He jogged down the sidewalk. She still wished that she could have parked it herself as she hated to see him go to so much trouble. She made sure she had a good tip ready for him when he came back. As he drove her car around she noticed how dusty it was. Maybe it took being at a nice hotel to realize that it was far overdue for a car wash. He handed her the keys and she gave him his tip. Once she was settled in the car she took a moment to send a text to her grandmother.

On my way home. I'm going to stop at the carwash. Be there soon.

Ally laughed as she wondered if having to wake up with Peaches and Arnold again had been a rude awakening for her grandmother. She drove back towards Blue River. The carwash she wanted to use was just inside town limits. It had a drive-through and an added drying feature. As she pulled into the carwash she noticed red and blue lights flashing behind her. She groaned.

"What did I do? Not use my signal?" She frowned and pulled to a stop. The patrol car stopped right behind her and turned off its lights. Ally reached into her purse for her license as the officer walked up to the door. She rolled down her window and looked right up into huge, hazel eyes framed by thick, dark lashes. Her heart skipped a beat. He looked even more handsome in uniform.

"Luke?" She grinned. "Are you going to write me a ticket?"

"Should I?" He quirked a brow and folded his arms. "I thought we were meeting for breakfast this morning?"

"Didn't you get my text?"

"No." He rested a hand on the door and met her eyes. "Did you cancel?"

"Yes. I thought I would have a bit too much to do today."

"Ah." He crouched down some. "Like going to the carwash?"

"Yes." She bit into her bottom lip.

"Good, because this thing is filthy." He laughed. Ally relaxed. She expected him to be frustrated, but he was just as easygoing as always. "I'm sorry if I scared you pulling up behind you like that. The chief wants to mix things up a bit so I'm on patrol today and I spotted you. You're not mad are you?"

"Well, I guess that depends on whether you're going to write me a ticket or not." She winked at him.

"I guess I could let it slide just this once. The boss frowns upon me writing tickets for women not showing up to breakfast."

"Oh? Are there many that stand you up?" Ally tilted her head to the side and smiled mischievously. Luke's smile faded and he met her eyes.

"Only one." He rapped the top of her door. "Enjoy your day."

"You too. Sorry about breakfast."

"It's all right, Ally. We'll figure it out one of these days." As he walked back to the patrol car she watched him in the rearview mirror.

Ally eased her car into the carwash and once it was on the tracks she relaxed. The whir and buzz of the machinery around her accompanied by the rush of water made her feel as if she had been transported to a different place, just like it had when she was a kid. Some of the things about moving back home to Blue River were very comforting to her, the carwash was one of them.

After Ally passed through the remainder of the carwash she headed for the cottage. She had promised her grandmother that she would help move a few more of her things from the cottage to Freely Lakes. She pulled into the driveway and the front door of the cottage flung open. Out came Arnold and Peaches, with Charlotte chasing after them. Ally laughed as she jumped out of the car and scooped up Peaches. Arnold nuzzled her shins and squealed. She reached down and patted his head.

"I guess I was missed."

"More than you could ever know. Do you realize that cat actually walked on my face this morning?"

"Oh Peaches, naughty." Ally clucked her tongue. "I'm sorry, Mee-Maw, they have been a little out of control since you've been gone."

"I see that. But it's okay, I enjoyed my time with them. Since she got me up early I was able to pack up the last of my things that I want to take over. If you're not too tired, can we get started?"

"Sure. Let me just put my overnight bag inside. I cleaned out the trunk before I left so there should be plenty of room in there for whatever we need to take." Ally wrapped her grandmother in a tight hug. "I still wish I was moving you back in."

"I know dear, I know."

Ally stepped into the cottage and walked through the living room to the small hall that led to the two bedrooms. She walked past the bedroom that she still considered to be her grandmother's then stepped into her own. It was the same bedroom she had grown up in. After she had moved out, her grandmother suggested that Ally take the larger room, but she just couldn't bring herself to do it. She loved her own room and it wouldn't feel right.

Ally dropped her overnight bag on her bed. She tucked her phone into her pocket and left her purse behind. Then she gathered up a stack of boxes from her grandmother's room to carry out to the car. They were fairly light, but she had a hard time seeing around them. She managed to make her way out the door.

"Wow, Ally let me take one of those." Charlotte reached for one of the boxes when Ally stepped outside.

"No, no. They're perfectly balanced. Could you pop the trunk, please?"

"Absolutely."

Ally walked around to the back of the car. She heard the subtle click of the release of the trunk and the whir of it rising. Only then did she set down the boxes on the ground. As she finished, she heard her grandmother scream.

"Mee-Maw? What is it?" Ally gasped. Charlotte pointed to the trunk of the car. Her hand trembled and another scream escaped her. Ally was filled with dread as she looked into the trunk. She stumbled back as she saw a man's body inside.

Chapter Three

Ally stared at the body in her trunk.

"Is he dead? He can't be dead. This has to be some kind of prank." She took a deep breath and tried to convince herself that the man might be sleeping or passed out. Ally's hand shook as she reached into the trunk. One touch of the man's wrist told her that he was dead, and had been for some time. His skin was cold. "I think he is dead." From the lump on his head and the telephone cord wrapped around his neck it was clear he had been murdered.

As Ally peered more closely at his face her heart dropped. "I know him. It's Dustin, the head of security at the hotel. How can he be dead in the trunk of my car? Why?" Ally noticed that the man was wrapped in a familiar jacket. It was the same jacket that Denise wore the day before. "I must be confused." She shook her head.

"Do you have any idea how he ended up in your trunk?" Charlotte stared at the man. "How did he get there, Ally?"

"I have no clue. I gave the keys to the valet when I arrived and I got the car back from the valet when I left. This is the first time I've opened the trunk." Ally reached for her phone. "I have to call Luke."

"Ally, listen to me." Charlotte grabbed the wrist of the hand that held the cell phone. "When you make that call you can't take it back."

"What do you mean?" Ally's eyes widened.

"Ally, honey, you have a dead man in the trunk of your car. The police are going to want some kind of explanation."

"But I don't have one. I don't know what happened." Ally gripped her phone tighter.

"I know that." Charlotte grimaced. "We have to call the police, but if you could remember anything that would indicate who did this it would be helpful. Did you see him fight with anyone? Was anyone following him?"

"No, not at all. He just seemed like a nice man. Mee-Maw, don't worry. Luke will make sure that I am okay." Ally dialed Luke's phone number. As it rang Charlotte herded the animals back into the house.

"Did you miss me already?"

"Luke." Her voice cracked.

"Ally, what is it? Where are you? What's wrong?"

"I'm in some trouble I think. I've got a big problem. I'm at the cottage."

"Are you hurt? What's going on?"

"I'm not hurt. But there's a body in the trunk of my car."

"A what? Did you say a body?"

"Luke please." Ally's eyes filled with tears as the full impact hit her.

"I'm sending help, I'll be there in five minutes."

"Luke wait, what do you mean you're sending help?"

"I'm going to call it in. I'm sure there's someone closer who will get there faster."

"Luke, I don't know. I don't know."

"It's going to be okay I'll be there in a few minutes. Just try to breathe."

Ally hung up the phone and looked back

towards the trunk. Her mind shifted into investigative mode. She checked over everything in the trunk. The only thing she noticed was a blue circular pin. It was the same pin she had seen on a few different jackets at the hotel. Obviously, whatever happened to Dustin happened at the hotel. But how could she prove that? What was she going to say to the officer that showed up? How could she explain something that she didn't understand herself?

Charlotte stepped back out of the house and hurried towards Ally. "What did Luke say?"

"He said he's sending help." A siren blared. Ally turned in the direction of it.

"Here it comes." Charlotte tightened her hands into fists. "Ally, all of this is going to happen fast. Be careful what you say, please?"

"Mee-Maw, don't worry, it's going to be fine," Ally said with more confidence than she felt.

A patrol car skidded to a stop at the end of the driveway. Ally grabbed her grandmother's hand as two officers walked up the driveway. Neither was Luke.

"You reported a body?" A tall, thin man she'd never seen before walked up to her.

"He's in the trunk." She took a step back from it.

"The trunk?" The officer tipped his head down as he looked inside. He checked for signs of life and then straightened up. When he looked at Ally his expression was stern. "Who owns this car?"

"I do." Ally cleared her throat.

"Do you know this man?"

"He's head of security at Bella Hotel in Mainbry. His name is Dustin Keeris." Charlotte placed a hand on her shoulder to remind her to be careful of what she said.

"Would you like to tell me how he ended up in the trunk of your car?" The officer shifted closer to her.

"I'd rather wait until Detective Luke Elm gets here."

"Oh?" He studied her. "Why do you want to wait for him?"

"I just think it would be better."

"So, you're withholding information from me

about this dead man in your trunk?" He rested his hand on his hip where handcuffs hung. Ally's chest tightened. She hadn't really considered what would happen after the police arrived. She heard the squeal of tires and glanced over. Luke leaped out of the car and rushed up the driveway.

"What's going on, Miller?" He placed a hand on Ally's shoulder. It tightened when he looked past her into the trunk and saw Dustin's body.

"You know this woman?" Miller asked.

"Yes, I do," Luke said.

"Well, maybe you can get her to tell you why she has a dead man who has obviously been murdered, in her trunk."

"Dustin. His name is Dustin." Her voice softened.

"Ally?" Luke stepped in front of her and looked into her eyes. "What happened?"

"I don't know. I opened the trunk to put these boxes in, and he was there."

"Where has the car been?" Luke looked back at the car.

"Just at the hotel. And the carwash when we

ran into each other. Remember?" Ally frowned.

"Wait, you took the car through a carwash with a body in the trunk?" Miller growled. "Do you realize that you washed away any evidence that might have been on the car?"

Ally stared at him. "I didn't know there was evidence then. I didn't know there was a body then."

"And you were with her?" Miller clenched his jaw. "You know how this is going to look don't you, Elm?"

Luke raised an eyebrow but didn't answer. His hand remained on Ally's shoulder, so tight that it seemed to her that he was trying to hold onto her.

"Look, I was with her, I know she didn't know about the body."

"You do?" Miller narrowed his eyes. "Or maybe, she let you know about the body and you suggested a carwash to help her out?"

"Watch it," Luke warned. "You better think about those accusations before you start throwing them around."

"Hey, hate me for saying what every other investigator on this case is going to say. I don't care. I can tell you right now, that you're going to have to come up with a better explanation than 'I don't know'."

"Luke?" Ally looked into his eyes. "Is he right? Are they going to arrest me?"

"No. Just let me handle this." His jaw rippled as he looked away from her.

"Sounds a little fishy to me." Miller spat on the driveway. Ally scrunched up her nose at the sight. A few more patrol cars pulled up followed by an unmarked car. As the officers assessed the scene, Ally's heart beat faster. Charlotte stood off to the side, but Ally felt her eyes on her.

"That's the new homicide detective, Ballantine," Luke whispered in her ear as he looked at a man walking towards them. He remained by her side as the investigation continued. When the detective walked up to them, Luke stepped slightly in front of Ally.

"This is your car, ma'am?" The detective was a short man with a round stomach and an ample amount of brown curls.

"Yes."

"And you say you were staying at Bella Hotel in Mainbry and that the valet parked your car which now has a dead body in it?"

"Yes." Ally leaned a little closer to Luke. "I have no idea how this happened."

"Well, maybe when you come down to the station with me, things will be a little clearer," Ballantine threatened. Luke moved in front of her.

"Why do you need to take her down to the station? She is cooperating with you."

"Look Elm, this isn't your case." The detective scowled at him. "And you will never be on it now we know you have a conflict of interest."

"I know." Luke clenched his jaw.

"Then why are you here?"

Luke dropped his gaze for a moment. He tightened his lips as he looked back up at the man. "It's obvious she didn't know the victim was in her trunk. Why would she call it in? Why would she have these boxes stacked up to go in the trunk?

How could she even physically get him in the trunk?"

"A lot of things about this situation don't make sense, Elm. Right now, I'm trying to figure out how you fit in."

Luke's posture tensed. "I'm here because Ally called me. I called it in to the police department and then came to offer support."

Ally reached into her pocket for her phone. "Here, just call Denise, the food and beverage manager at the hotel. She'll confirm that I was there, why I was there. Really, that's all you have to do." Ally's voice shook as she tried to reason with the detective.

"That's going to magically make the dead body disappear?" Ballantine took the phone from her. "I don't think you understand the situation here, Ms. Sweet. You are the last person who had contact with this man."

"No, I'm not, I'm certainly not. I mean, I only saw him in the early evening, and then not again after that."

"Ally, careful." Charlotte stepped up beside

her. "There's no need to explain yourself without a lawyer. You had nothing to do with this."

"Mee-Maw, I am telling the truth. There's no reason to hide that."

"You're absolutely right." The detective looked towards Charlotte with a withering glare. "Unless there's something that you're afraid she'll say."

"I don't trust you not to take what she says and twist it." Charlotte met his eyes boldly. "She has the right to a lawyer."

"You think she needs one?" The detective smirked. "That's good to know. You send one on down to the station to meet us there."

"That's not necessary." Luke cleared his throat. "You're new here, Ballantine. I might not be able to pull rank on you, but I have connections in this town and advise that you listen to my opinion. I know what you're doing, and there's no need to strong arm her. She's been traumatized by this. She lives here and operates a business here. She is not a flight risk. There is no reason to take her into custody."

"Simmer down there, young stallion." Ballantine laughed so loud that a bit of spit flew out of his mouth. "No one said anything about custody. I was looking forward to a friendly conversation." His laughter faded as abruptly as it started. "Are you threatening me, Detective?"

Luke looked away from him and grimaced. "No Sir. I just think that this is a delicate situation that should be handled in a delicate manner."

"Sure. She looks real delicate." Ballantine winked at Ally. Ally shied back closer to Luke. She was certain he had stepped out of line by speaking to Ballantine that way, but she was impressed by his boldness. Luke glared at him in response to his comment. "Elm, I'm not going to take her in right now. I'm going to leave her under your watchful eye. That doesn't mean that I won't arrest her if her story doesn't check out. Make sure she doesn't go missing, understand?"

"Yes Sir." Luke nodded. Ally had to bite into her bottom lip to keep from telling the detective what she thought of him. She was grateful that she wasn't cuffed, but not happy with his attitude towards her or Luke.

"If you want me to come down to the station I will." She pulled away from Luke. "I have nothing to hide."

"No, you won't." Luke grabbed her by the hand and held it tight. "This is fine. He'll check things out, and you'll be fine, Ally."

Detective Ballantine's phone buzzed. He handed Ally back her phone while he checked his own.

"Oops, it looks like it might not be up to me much longer. Mainbry is likely to take over the case since it's believed the murder took place at the hotel. However, I'm sure there will be a bit of go-between." He looked up at Luke. "Don't expect special treatment for your delicate friend here from the Mainbry homicide detective. They're pretty by the book."

"I know." Luke nodded and watched him as he walked away. Ally was very aware that his hand was still grasping hers.

"Luke, you didn't have to do that. You don't have to stand up for me."

He turned to look at her, his expression grim. "I did what I thought was right, Ally. You have to trust me on these things. The moment he had you in an interrogation room I wouldn't have been able to help you. As long as you are out, we have options."

"Options?" Ally searched his eyes.

"We don't need to worry about that now." He turned her towards the cottage. "Let's go inside while they process the crime scene."

"No Luke, I don't want to go inside. I have to go back to the hotel. I have to talk to Denise." She turned towards Charlotte. "Mee-Maw, can I take the van?"

"Wait a second, you're not going anywhere." Luke crossed his arms.

"What?" Ally spun around to look at him. "Luke, there was a dead man in my trunk. I have to find out what really happened, and fast. What if they come back for me?"

"Hey, you don't have to worry. All right?" Luke met her eyes. "I'm not going to let anything happen to you."

"Thank you, Luke, but the last thing I need right now is a babysitter." Ally turned back to Charlotte who held out the keys to the van. Luke intercepted them and took them right out of Charlotte's hand.

"Sorry Ally, but that's exactly what you have. Until we know more about what happened here, you're stuck with me."

"Luke." She looked into his eyes.

"Ally." He quirked his brow. She sighed.

"Well, then come with me. I'll even let you drive."

"I don't know if that's a good idea, Ally. The hotel is going to be crawling with investigators. Let's just give it a little time. All right? Let's go inside for a few minutes and think this through."

"All right, but not for long. I want to get ahead of this before it gets out of control."

"Ally, it's under control." Charlotte patted her back. "Don't worry we'll figure this out."

Chapter Four

Luke opened the door to the cottage for both Ally and her grandmother. Once inside, Ally began to pace. She couldn't stop herself from moving as she felt a strong urge to run. Peaches lay on the couch and Arnold lay on the rug. They both watched her as if sensing she needed room.

"Luke, let me get you some tea. We'll let Ally calm down for a few minutes, okay?" Charlotte looked past him and met Ally's eye. Ally nodded. Luke followed after Charlotte into the kitchen. As soon as he was gone, Ally reached into her pocket and pulled out her phone. She dialed Denise's number. With every ring she grew more anxious.

"Hello, this is Denise."

"Denise, it's Ally. Listen to me, the police are on the way there to question you. I found Dustin dead in the trunk of my car." She stumbled over her words as she spoke too fast to make herself clear.

"What? Dustin's dead? Are you sure?"

"Yes, I am."

"But why was he in your trunk? Ally, what is going on?"

"I don't know, Denise. But you have to know I had nothing to do with this. I would never hurt anyone."

"I do know that. I do, Ally, of course. But how can this be happening?"

"I don't know, but I'm going to have to figure it out and I think I need your help. Someone murdered Dustin and put him in my trunk for a reason. It must be personal."

"I'm sure the police can get to the bottom of it."

"I'm not so sure. Unfortunately, I think they already feel they have. They think I was involved. My friend, Luke, is the only reason I'm not down at the station right now."

"Oh Ally, that can't be true. There's no way they can prove you did something that you didn't do."

"I can't take the risk. I need to try and find out the truth myself. This is serious. And there's something else." Ally paused a moment and took a breath. "Dustin was wrapped in your jacket, Denise. The one that you had on yesterday. How could that be?"

"What? Really?" She paused for a moment. "I don't know. I really don't. It had a stain on it so I left it in the laundry last night before I went home. Do you think the police will know it's mine?"

"I'm not sure, but they will probably find out. I'm worried. I just didn't want you to be surprised when the police arrived."

"Oh Ally, they're here, I have to go."

"Denise?" She winced as the line cut off.

"Ally? What are you doing? Who were you talking to?" Luke set down his cup of tea on the coffee table as Ally hung up the phone.

"Denise." Her breath escaped her as she saw the frustration in his expression.

"What? Why would you call her? Are you trying to make this easy on Ballantine?"

"I just didn't want her to be surprised by the police." Ally shrugged and looked away. "What's the problem?"

"You shouldn't have done that, Ally."

"She had to hang up because the police were there to talk to her. I'll call her back in a few minutes and see how it went."

"Ally!" Luke took her phone out of her hand. "Are you ever going to trust me enough to listen to my advice?"

Startled by his frustration, Ally took a step back. "I'm sorry, I'm a little out of it, Luke. I didn't mean to upset you. Why is a phone call such a big deal?"

"The problem is that now you are conspiring with someone at the hotel. Ally, can't you see that you have to be careful right now? You can't just do whatever you want." Luke ran his hand back through his hair and groaned. "This is just getting worse. These things have a way of snowballing, you have to calculate your every move."

"Luke, I didn't kill Dustin, so I shouldn't have anything to worry about."

"I wish that were the case, Ally. But someone put that body in your trunk. Someone is probably trying to frame you." He balled his hands into fists. "I don't tell you things for no reason, Ally.

You have to let me protect you, or you're going to end up in jail."

"That's why I want to go to the hotel, to find out what really happened, Luke. I know that you want to protect me, but I know that will only go so far."

"I know you're scared, but this is not the time to make any mistakes. Look, the truth is, me meeting you at the carwash makes it look like I might have helped you hide the evidence. We're in this together, and I need to know that you're as interested in protecting me as I am in protecting you." He sighed and handed her back her phone. "I'm sorry I just want you to be careful."

"No, you're right." Ally tightened her grip on her phone. "I can't think clearly about anything right now. All I want to do is go to that hotel and find out the truth. Am I really supposed to sit here and wait to see what happens? What if they find some reason to think that I am responsible for his death?"

"We can only take it one step at a time. We don't have any control over what happens next."

"I do." Ally stared into his eyes. "Luke, I don't want to go against your wishes. I respect you, and your experience, you know that. But this is my life we're talking about. I don't want to go to prison."

"Ally, I'm not going to let that..."

"But you can't stop it, can you?" Ally shook her head. "If they find more evidence, which they might if someone is framing me, they're not going to hesitate to blame me for the murder. Then it will be too late. I have to go down there and find out something, anything, that will clear my name."

Luke reached out and ran his hands along the curve of her shoulders. "Try to calm down. You're talking about interfering with an investigation and putting yourself at even more risk."

"I am calm." Ally stepped back from him. "If you really thought about this you'd see that it's my only option. I have no alibi, I was alone in my hotel room, the body was in my car. What jury is going to believe that I'm innocent?"

"But you have no motive, there's no reason for you to have killed Dustin."

"That doesn't mean much. Does it, Luke? How many people have you put behind bars that had no motive?"

"Ally." He closed his eyes and pinched the bridge of his nose.

"You know I'm right, Luke. This might be my only chance to clear my name. I'll just go..."

"You're not going anywhere." He opened his eyes again and stepped towards her in the same moment. "Not without me."

"I can't ask you to put yourself at even more risk, Luke."

"My reputation is on the line here, too. If this is what you're determined to do, then I will go with you. But you have to understand that if you get caught, the consequences could be dire. You might be arrested on the spot."

Ally looked away at the thought. "I know. But I need to get to the bottom of this, before it's too late."

"All right. Then you and I will go together to the hotel. I want you to promise me that you're not going to try to go off on your own. Can you do that?" He met her eyes.

"Yes, I promise."

"Really?"

"Yes Luke. Please can we go?"

His jaw rippled and he looked up at the ceiling. She could tell that he was going against his instincts. "Yes, let's go. We'll take my car."

"Be careful, please." Charlotte stepped into the living room. Ally assumed she was listening from the hall.

"I suppose you think this is a good idea, too?" Luke asked.

"You can't leave your fate to other people, Luke. She's right. The situation isn't good, and the more information we have the better off you will both be. I don't want Ally to be in danger any more than you do, but I think she needs to take action now. Before it's too late, don't you think?"

Luke lowered his eyes and nodded. "I guess you're right."

"Just be careful." Charlotte patted his chest. "I don't want you to get in trouble, Luke, and I want both of you to come back unscathed."

"Mee-Maw, we'll be fine."

"We'll be careful." Luke nodded.

Chapter Five

Luke led Ally out of the cottage and to his car. He opened the trunk and took out two pairs of sunglasses and two baseball caps. He handed them to Ally.

"So we can be a bit incognito." He winked.

"Always prepared." Ally smiled as they got into the car.

Luke started the car. As they drove down the road towards Mainbry, Ally found it hard not to fidget. After a few minutes of silence she looked over at Luke.

"I'm sorry, you know. I really am. I never would have involved you in this."

"Don't say that." He looked over at her, then back at the road.

"Why?"

"Because it's not your fault. I expect you to involve me in anything that puts you at risk. Ally, I know we haven't known each other that long, maybe that's why you don't understand that when I say I'm here for you I mean it. It's not just something I say." He turned a corner and then looked over at her again. Ally's cheeks burned as she looked down at her hands.

Ally's attention was drawn by the large amount of police cars in the parking lot of the hotel. Luke drove past. He parked at the grocery store a few blocks down from the hotel.

"Maybe you were right, Luke. How are we going to get past all of those officers?"

"There's always a back way." They each put on a pair of sunglasses and a baseball cap. Ally tucked her long, brown hair into the cap. She was surprised at how well the caps and sunglasses hid their features. They stepped out of the car. "Just try to act casual." He slid his hand into hers without hesitation. Ally glanced over at him, but his eyes remained trained on the sidewalk. As they walked towards the hotel, Luke tilted his head towards the building.

"I want you to tell me everything that happened when you arrived."

"I gave my keys to the valet. I didn't want to. I asked him if I could just park it somewhere, but he insisted. So, I gave him my keys and overnight bag. Then as I was walking into the hotel, I almost bumped into Dustin. He introduced himself and took me to Denise."

"Did he mention anything else to you that might have stood out?" Luke steered her along a maintenance driveway that led to a rear door of the hotel.

"He said he was spending the night at the hotel to test out the security."

"Hm." Luke quirked a brow. "Guess it wasn't great."

"I guess not." Ally paused when Luke held up his hand to her. He opened the maintenance door a crack so that he could peer into the hotel. "All clear," he said softly and gestured for her to step inside. "Anything else you can remember? Anything Denise mentioned?"

"No nothing." Ally shook her head. "Like I said, I barely spoke to Dustin."

"But the valet insisted on taking the car keys," Luke asked in a hushed voice.

"Yes. And he had that same pin on that we

found in the trunk. But so did a few other staff members I saw," Ally said softly.

"Hm. Did Denise have one?"

"No." She cringed as she recalled the jacket that the body was wrapped in. "Luke, I have to tell you something, but I want you to hear everything I have to say first."

"What?" His expression stiffened, but his voice remained soft.

"The jacket that Dustin was wrapped in, I recognized it."

"What do you mean?" He turned to face her fully.

"I have known Denise for a long time, and she would never do anything to hurt anyone. But that was her jacket."

"What? And you didn't think to tell me this before? Ally, we could have avoided all of this!" Luke frowned and ran his hand back through his hair. "Why didn't you tell me?"

"Because, I know Denise didn't do it." Ally tried to keep her voice low even though she was upset. "If I told the detective about it, he would have thought she was involved."

"Ally, they're going to figure out it's her jacket either way. If we had told them, it would have made your case look a little better."

"I wouldn't want to do that. Denise is just as innocent as I am." Ally crossed her arms and regarded him with irritation. "I want you to believe me."

"I'm sorry, but the only thing that I believe right now, is that you didn't do this, which means we need to prove that someone else did."

"Not Denise." She shook her head.

"Sh." Luke looked down the hall. "Someone's coming. Here." He pulled open a door and tugged her inside. The space was rather small. Ally was pinned against the wall, while Luke did his best not to flatten her against it. "Sh."

She nodded. In the hall she could hear a male and a female voice. It took her a moment to recognize that the female voice belonged to Lisa, the maid that was in charge of distributing the chocolates for the turndown service.

"So, you're saying she asked you to give him

two specific candies?" The man asked.

"Yes. I thought it was a little strange, but she said it was because he didn't like mint or dark chocolate."

"But she claims never to have met him before yesterday. How would she know that?"

"I don't know, Detective. I just did what she asked and put the candies in his room."

Ally didn't recognize his voice so she presumed he was the Mainbry detective. A cell phone rang outside the door. "I just have to take this," the detective said.

"Is that true? Did you give him special chocolates?" Luke whispered as he met her eyes.

"He didn't like mint or dark chocolate. He told me when I met him and offered him a chocolate. I just asked the maid to make sure that he got the caramel ones on his pillow." She braced herself against the wall as Luke leaned closer to her.

"That doesn't look good. It looks like you had a personal connection to him." He paused a moment, then took a breath. "Did you?"

"What?" She narrowed her eyes, speaking as

quietly as possible.

"Did you have a personal relationship with him? Maybe you flirted, maybe you spent some time talking after your meeting with Denise? Anything like that?"

"Luke, no." Ally shook her head. "Not at all."

"I'm only asking because if you lie about it, it will only make things worse for you, Ally."

"I'm not lying." She closed her eyes for a moment. "I barely spoke to him. He showed me to Denise, then I met with Denise, and that was it."

He nodded.

"Sorry about that," the detective continued talking in the corridor.

Luke put his finger to his lips as the pair stopped outside the door.

"Did you notice anything strange in his room while you were there? Anything out of order?" The detective asked.

"Nothing strange, he just had no dry towels left when I checked the room so I asked the maid that works the floor to leave fresh towels. When I bumped into her later she had two of the hotel wine glasses on her from his room, they must have been left there after I had left the chocolates. I took the glasses from her."

"Why did you take them?"

"I've become quite friendly with her and she asked me to help her out because I was going downstairs. One of the glasses had lipstick on it, and that's tough to get off the glass if it sits too long."

"Where are the glasses now?"

"In the kitchen I presume. They would have been washed last night."

"Great." The detective sighed. "So, he had a female guest. Had you noticed him with anyone?"

"I'm sorry, Sir, I only started last week. That's why I have this pin, I'm still in training. They put me in charge of the turndown service because I did it at another hotel in the city. I'm not that familiar with the people that work here."

Ally bit into her bottom lip. So that was what the pin meant. It also meant that whoever left the pin in the trunk was likely a trainee. Which might make it easier to narrow down. Lisa still had hers, but that didn't rule her out. Maybe she asked for a new one. She was determined to check with Denise about it. The voices faded as the pair walked away. Luke remained close to her. She tried not to think about how heavy her heart pounded against her chest. If she let herself get caught up in it, she might get too distracted to figure out the truth.

"Do you think it's safe yet?"

"In a hurry to get away from me?" Luke leaned a little closer with a sly smile.

"Luke."

"Okay, okay." With a quiet motion he opened the door. He checked the hall again, then gestured for Ally to follow him. As they headed down the hall, Ally wondered if Luke doubted her. The way he had looked at her, made her think that he wasn't sure if she was telling the truth. If even he wasn't convinced, then why would the police believe her? As they neared the main lobby Ally heard a familiar voice.

"That's Denise," she said softly.

"Are you sure?"

Ally nodded. Luke peeked around the entrance to the lobby. Ally did as well. She saw a man who stood very close to Denise.

"I had nothing to do with this," Denise said.

"No? Because I have just heard from my partner that there were two wine glasses in the victim's room. One with lipstick. I would guess it matches that lovely shade you have on."

"No." Denise shook her head. "I never saw Dustin that night. I went home."

"But no one can prove that?"

"I live alone."

"No boyfriend?"

"Not right now." She cleared her throat.

"Not since you and Dustin broke up?"

Ally ducked her head back. Her heart pounded as she listened for Denise's answer.

"Yes, we were dating. But it's been over for almost two weeks."

"That's not very long. Maybe he invited you into his room to talk about things. Maybe you forced your way in. Emotions ran high, and he ended up dead?"

"No! I did not go in his room. I was at home. We were fine with the breakup. We were still friends."

"It isn't very friendly to murder someone."

"That's ridiculous."

"Is it? Several of the staff here have informed myself and my partner that you and Dustin had some rather loud verbal altercations."

"That was before we broke up. He wanted to continue things, I told him we couldn't because I took this job. They don't allow dating between personnel and security, it's too much of a risk. He wanted to continue in secret, but I didn't. As soon as I made that clear we didn't argue anymore."

"But maybe he wasn't satisfied with your decision? Did he come after you? Hurt you?"

"No, he was a good friend. You don't have any proof, if you did, I would be in custody."

"Good idea. I think that we're ready to take that step. We know a few things. You have a motive, you had the opportunity, and you just happened to conceal the body in the trunk of a car that belongs to a friend of yours. Maybe she told you she would get rid of it? I guess she didn't turn out to be such a great friend after all." He held out his handcuffs. "Now, are you going to make a scene?"

Ally tensed. Luke put his hand on her arm to hold her back from pushing past him. He shot her a stern look.

"Don't," Luke said firmly, but he kept his voice quiet.

"I have to help her," Ally pleaded.

"Ally don't." When she started to pull away from him, he grabbed her by the crook of her elbow. "You promised. Remember?"

All of her defiance deflated. Luke was right. There was nothing she could do to help Denise in that moment. But if she revealed that she and Luke were there, then there would be a lot of questions to answer. Still, it was hard for Ally to watch the officer lead Denise out of the hotel to a waiting patrol car.

"She didn't do this, Luke. I know she didn't."

"It's been a long time since the last time you saw her, hasn't it? Maybe she's changed, Ally. Life and stress can do a lot of crazy things to you. Or maybe, like the detective said, Dustin put her in an impossible position."

"But how would killing Dustin benefit her?"

"Maybe she just lost it."

"They seemed to get along."

"You never know what's happening beneath the surface." Luke's jaw rippled.

"In your experience?"

"Yes, experience has shown me that you never know what goes on behind closed doors."

"Maybe you're right, Luke, but I don't know. None of it makes sense. It just doesn't add up."

"It will, we just have to be patient."

Ally nodded, even though that seemed like the worst possible path to take. Luke's phone vibrated. He glanced at the screen and frowned.

"I'm being called in."

"Don't they know that you're babysitting?" Ally smiled a little in an attempt to lighten the mood.

"I don't think I need to anymore, since Mainbry has a suspect in custody."

"So she goes to jail, and I'm free?"

Luke met her eyes. "I didn't know my company was such torture."

"It's not." Ally glanced away. "Not at all."

"I have to go, Ally. I can't ignore a request. The best place for you right now is at home with Charlotte. I know she'll keep you out of trouble."

Ally tried not to smile at that. Maybe Luke was getting to know her pretty well but he clearly had no idea what Charlotte was really like. "Luke, it's fine, I'll be fine. Let's just get back to the cottage. There's nothing more we can do here." He stared at her.

"You're not going to fight me?" Luke asked softly.

"No, I think you're right. Like you said we can't be caught here. There is not really anything that can be done to help Denise right now." Ally shrugged. "I want to check on Mee-Maw and make sure that she's not too upset."

"Good idea," Luke said and then checked to make sure the hall was clear. He then led her back towards the maintenance entrance. Once they were outside again Ally felt a sense of relief. A tension left her that she didn't even realize was there until it was gone.

"Are you okay, Ally?" Luke put an arm around her shoulders as they walked. Ally stole a look in his direction, but looked away before he caught her.

"I think so."

"You're strong. You know that?"

"You think so?"

"Sure. Most people in your situation would have lost it or given up. You have such a problem solving mentality. Maybe it gets you, okay both of us, into trouble at times, but it's a very valuable thing to have."

"Thanks Luke." She smiled. They reached the car and he opened the door for her.

"When this is all over, you owe me breakfast, remember?" Luke said. He grinned and closed the door. When he settled into the driver's seat Ally did her best not to let him see the blush in her cheeks. She knew that he was determined, and that thrilled her. But she was also determined not to be in a position that she did not feel comfortable in. As Luke's friend, she was very comfortable. If their friendship became anything more than that she had no idea how she would feel. When they reached the cottage Luke pulled the car up outside the front.

"I will find out what I can about the case and meet you back here as soon as I can. If anything happens call me right away. Understand?" He looked into her eyes intently. "Just try to relax, I'll do what I can to help you."

"Thanks Luke. That means a lot to me." She leaned over and kissed his cheek. Her heart fluttered at the contact. His eyes widened. He tipped his head as if he might kiss her in return. Instead he smiled.

"I'll see you later. Take care," he said as Ally got out of the car.

After Luke had driven off Ally opened the door to the cottage and was greeted by Peaches who wound around her legs with such speed and excitement that Ally nearly tripped. Ally reached down and stroked the cat from head to tail. When she straightened up again she was face to face with her grandmother.

"Ally, I was worried. How did it go?"

Ally's lips tightened into a grim line. "They arrested Denise."

"What? Why?" Charlotte's eyes grew wide.

"Apparently she was in a relationship with Dustin. A maid found two wine glasses in his room. One with lipstick. I guess the police think that she was with him shortly before he was killed, and was probably the one to kill him."

"Oh no, I couldn't imagine that being true. She is a very kind woman." Charlotte wrung her hands. "This is insane. First it was you, now Denise."

"I know. I don't believe it either. I saw the two of them together and they were very friendly to each other. There didn't seem to be any problems between them. How could they go from that to murder in just a few hours?"

"Even if something did happen, maybe he attacked her, maybe she defended herself and things got out of control, why would she put the body in your trunk?"

Ally gazed out the front window of the cottage. "I don't know. Unless maybe she hoped I would help her. But why wouldn't she have said something to me when I called her?"

"I don't think she did this, Ally." Charlotte raised an eyebrow. "Where's Luke?"

"He got called in to work. I'm on my own. Which is why we need to figure out a way to get into the crime scene. If we wait too long any clues that we might find will be gone."

"I don't think we can, Ally, they took your car."

"Not that crime scene. Dustin wasn't killed in my trunk. Someone put his body there. Which means that he had to have been killed at the hotel. Maybe in his room? If we can get in there we might be able to find a clue as to who the killer is."

"But the place will be flooded with police. How will we get past?"

"I'm not sure." Ally sighed. "But we have to do something. I have to help Denise."

"I think it's worth a try. But it will be difficult,"

Charlotte replied.

"The first step is getting there."

"Let me just feed Arnold and Peaches, or we might come home to a torn up cottage."

"Good point." Ally nodded. "I'm going to change. I should have changed even before I went to the hotel with Luke. It will be harder for people to recognize me if I'm in different clothes. I'll just be a minute."

Ally stepped into her bedroom and to her surprise Peaches followed after her. Normally the cat would race into the kitchen to get food. "Aw honey, you're worried about me aren't you?" Ally scooped her up and snuggled her close to her cheek. "I know, you can tell I'm upset. But everything is going to be okay. I just have to get a few things straightened out. Go eat." Ally put her back down on the floor. Peaches gave her a forlorn look, then took off at the sound of the can opener. Ally laughed as she gathered some clothes to change into. Though Peaches was a cat, Ally considered her to be her closest friend. Once she was changed she grabbed a pair of gloves, put them in her pocket and met her grandmother in the living room.

"I'm taking some chocolates with us," Charlotte said as she held up a box of chocolates. "That way if we are caught we have an excuse for being there."

"Good thinking." Ally smiled as she placed a hat on her head and handed a shawl to her grandmother so she could tie it around her head and be less recognizable. "Let's head out. If Luke comes back before we go, he might not want us to follow through."

"Might not, Ally?" Charlotte's eyes shone. "I think you know better than that."

"Plausible deniability, Mee-Maw. It's important."

"You might consider that Luke knows what he is talking about. Getting involved in this, especially when you are probably still on the suspect list, is a big risk."

"I know. But I'm still going to do what I can. I think Mom would have done the same for Denise."

"You're right." Charlotte smiled fondly. "She was just as brave and stubborn as you."

Ally's heart swelled at the thought of being similar to her mother.

Chapter Six

As Ally and Charlotte started driving towards the hotel Ally's nerves began to rattle. Were they really going to break into a crime scene? She tried not to think about the consequences. To distract herself she glanced over at her grandmother.

"Mee-Maw, does Rose know that Denise was arrested?"

"I don't know. She will be so upset. Denise is her only daughter and they have always been so close. She hasn't been well lately. I'm a little worried about her health. It might be best to try to keep her out of this until it all settles down."

"Yes, this might be too upsetting. But I wonder if she might know something that could help us."

"Let's see what we turn up first, then we'll think about talking to Rose."

"Okay," Ally agreed.

Ally parked the van in the same spot that Luke had parked in earlier. Then they made their way to the same back door. Charlotte held onto the chocolate box. Ally checked to see if the path was clear then held open the door for her grandmother. As they walked down the hall, Charlotte stuck right by her side.

"Remember, if anything goes wrong, you run, and I'll distract."

"Nothing is going to go wrong, Mee-Maw. Not as long as we're careful."

"How are we even going to find out what room he was staying in?" Charlotte paused at the end of the hall. Ally tilted her head towards a group of people that were gathered together at the front desk.

"Let's see if they mention it, otherwise we'll see if we can find the door with the police tape on."

Ally walked towards the front desk at a casual pace. She did her best to look as if she belonged there. She stopped a few steps away from the group which was a mixture of people in the hotel's uniform, and people in plain clothes.

"I can't believe he's dead." A man that she recognized as the valet that took her car and returned it, shook his head. "The lady gave me a nice tip and everything. I never would have thought she would do something like this. I guess you never can tell. I should have suspected something when she wanted to park her own car." He shuddered. "I can't believe I was in the same car as a dead body."

"Hey, that dead body is Dustin." A maid spoke up. "We should show some respect. This wasn't just some event that happened. This was a member of our staff. I feel terrible for Dustin. I warned him that he should have let things go with Denise."

"Please, Denise didn't have anything to do with this," Lisa said. "That much I know for sure. She's never been anything but nice to me."

"You didn't break her heart." Another member of staff shook his head. "Maybe she wanted to get a little revenge."

"Or maybe Dustin thought he was going to get a reunion with her. Either way, it's pretty clear that she had to be involved. Why would some random person just murder Dustin?"

"We don't know that much about his past. It could have been someone that had nothing to do with the hotel." The valet winced. "What I think is that once we have access we need to make sure that room 312 gets a good scrub down."

"Sure, I bet you'd like to help with that?" The maid raised an eyebrow. "The last thing I want to do is go in that room."

"All of you need to get back to work." A man walked towards the group from the other side. Ally almost didn't notice him as she was so caught up in the conversation. She backed up a little as he paused in front of the group. "We're not here to chit chat. What happened was horrible, but we still have a hotel to run. If any of you have a problem with that, you're welcome to leave. But don't expect your jobs to be here when you come back."

"Ben, don't you think that's a little harsh? I mean, we might need time to grieve." The woman from behind the front desk frowned.

"Kylie, you're welcome to grieve all you want, but it's not going to be here, and not on my dollar.

All of you back to your posts."

"What if the police want to speak to us again?" The valet looked a little nervous.

"Don't worry about them, Tim. I'll handle the police from now on. Go on."

Ally backed away before the group dispersed. She didn't want Ben, who she assumed was the manager to see her. She wondered if he would even still want to come out to the shop after what had happened. When she returned to Charlotte she whispered in her ear.

"Room 312."

"Who was that guy that walked up to the group?" Charlotte asked softly.

"I think it must be the manager. I didn't have a chance to meet him this morning, but I guess he got called in after all this happened. Let's see if we can find an elevator that's not in the lobby."

"I think I saw one when we were coming in, near the kitchen. Back here." Charlotte led Ally back towards the kitchen area. Ally wondered if the two glasses that were found in Dustin's room were really from Denise and Dustin. Was she lying about meeting him? Or did he have a drink with someone else? Just as they were about to pass the kitchen, Ally heard a voice call out.

"Make sure you get those strawberries up to 217, I told them they would be there in ten minutes. I wrote it on the list. Check the list!"

The person sounded pretty aggravated, but Ally didn't care about that, her focus was on what he had said. The list. If someone had wine sent up to room 312, then wouldn't it be on that list? She glanced over at her grandmother.

"Wait just a minute, I want to see if I can get into the kitchen."

"I can create a diversion?" Charlotte smiled.

"Perfect."

"You stay in the corner there. I'll draw them out through the other door. Then slip in and slip out. I'll try to distract as long as I can."

"Okay." Ally met her grandmother's eyes. "Be careful."

Ally waited in the corner as her grandmother had instructed. Charlotte walked further down the hall to the open second door that led into the kitchen. She paused right beside it, and let out a yell. Ally was startled by just how loud her grandmother could be. She didn't hesitate to slip inside the kitchen though. Just as she slipped in she caught sight of the kitchen staff rushing out to the hallway. Ally had to think fast. She assumed that the list might be by the phone. But would it still have orders from the night before on it? She wasn't sure. She did find a notepad by the phone, but it was blank. Her heart dropped. Her idea was worthless. But as the commotion continued outside of the kitchen she decided to look in one other place. The refrigerator. It was where she would keep a list.

When she walked up to the large, stainless steel refrigerator she saw there was a big piece of paper on it that was attached to the refrigerator with a magnet. The paper had dates sectioned off, including the day before. Ally read over the list quickly. There were people that requested everything from whipped cream to caviar, and several requests for wine. She ran her finger down the wine requests and found several room numbers. However, room 312 was not one of them. In fact room 312 hadn't placed any orders that were recorded on the list the day before. Ally heard a pronounced burp from outside in the hall.

"Oh dear, excuse me, I'm so sorry. It must have been indigestion. Here I thought I was having a heart attack," Charlotte said. "Thank you so much for coming to my aid."

"No problem, ma'am. Are you sure you don't want us to call an ambulance?"

"No, please, I'm embarrassed enough. I just had a little too much good food on my vacation."

Ally stepped out into the hall as the kitchen staff returned to the kitchen. She couldn't help but grin at her grandmother's subtle bow.

"Nice. A burp and everything?" Ally laughed quietly.

"I take acting very seriously. Did you find anything?"

"No. No orders at all from room 312. If Dustin had wine with someone, it doesn't seem like the wine came from his room. Unless of course he picked it up himself."

"That's all right, it's one more piece of the puzzle to figure out. Let's get up to the room and see if there is anything to find there."

"Let's take the elevator." Ally walked over to it and pushed the button. The doors slid open and a man brushed past her. She could see the angry grimace on his face. He held an envelope in one hand and his keys in the other. Ally shivered a little as she stepped into the elevator. Just when the doors began to slide shut, Ally caught sight of Ben, the manager of the hotel, and the man that had brushed past her. They stopped in the middle of the lobby.

"Thanks for nothing." The man held up an envelope and then stormed towards the door. The elevator doors closed all the way before Ally could see Ben's reaction.

"That was interesting." Ally nudged Charlotte with her elbow. "I wonder what it was about?"

"Not sure. We'll have to try to find out." The elevator doors opened again on the third floor. Ally led the way down the hall.

"This is the room," Ally said as she paused

outside room 312.

"I'm surprised it doesn't have crime scene tape across it. Maybe the manager requested that it didn't so as to create less of a scene for the other guests," Charlotte said as she reached out and tried the knob. "It's locked."

"Great. We can't go through the window, it's on the third floor. How are we going to get in?" Ally's attention was drawn by the sound of the elevator doors. Ally waved her grandmother up against the wall. "I wonder if they will give us a discount for all of this." Ally met her grandmother's eyes.

"I'm not sure. I would think that they might. After all, this was a very unpleasant experience," Charlotte said following Ally's lead.

The two continued their conversation as a couple walked past them. The man used a key to open one of the doors further up the hall. Once they were inside the room Ally smiled.

"I know how we're going to get in. We'll get the key," Ally said.

"How?"

"They're behind the front desk." Ally smiled.

"I doubt the key for the room is behind the desk. We need a master key. Most of the staff would have one."

"I saw Dustin give a staff member a master key and she put it behind the front desk. Maybe the key for room 312 or a master key is behind the front desk. They might be easy to access. The only problem is that I can't be the one to access it."

"I can do it, Ally." Charlotte smiled with confidence.

"Are you sure? It might get hectic if you get caught."

"Don't worry, I can handle it." They walked towards the elevator.

"What are you going to do?" Ally asked as the doors opened.

"Ally, please stop. You do realize that you get your snooping skills from me, don't you?" They got in the elevator and went down to the ground floor.

"Yes." Ally smiled. The elevator doors slid open.

"You stay out of sight, I'll get the key," Charlotte said.

"Okay. But I'll be watching."

"That's good. You can take notes." Charlotte smiled mischievously as she turned to walk over to the front desk. Ally ducked into a short corridor beside the elevator and watched as her grandmother paused at the front counter. She leaned on it and looked around as if she might be lost. When Kylie turned to look at her, she smiled widely.

"How can I help you?"

"Well, I'm afraid I've misplaced my key." She sighed. "I know, I know, I shouldn't lose things so easily, but it was here and then it was gone. In fact I think I might have left it at the front desk."

"What room are you in ma'am?"

"I'm in room 203, no 301, oh dear. Wait just a minute." She tapped her finger on the counter.

"Ma'am, if you could just tell me your name then I could look up which room you're in."

"Oh no, I need to remember this. Just give me a second." Charlotte looked thoughtful.

"Let's see what keys are loose back here. 315?" She picked up a key.

"Oh yes, that's it!" Charlotte reached for the key. Kylie handed it to her. The moment Charlotte had it in her hand she let it slip out of her grasp. "Oh dear, here I go again." She reached behind the counter for the key that Kylie did not pick up. She hoped it was a master key or the one to Dustin's room.

"I'll get it, I'll get it." Kylie tried to shoo her hand out from behind the counter, but Charlotte already had the key in her hand.

"There we are, thank you so much, dear. I appreciate it."

"Anything you need." Kylie nodded at her, then looked back at her computer. Ally grinned at Charlotte as she walked back towards her with the key in hand.

"I think this might get us in." She held it up in the air. "But we have to hurry. You never know when she might notice that it's missing. Catch the elevator." She pointed to the doors that were about to close. Ally sprinted down the hall to catch it, then held the doors for her grandmother. Charlotte stepped into the elevator.

Ally nodded. "Let's make this quick and neat. No one has to know we were ever there." Ally hit the button for the third floor.

"No one, like Luke?"

"I don't have to answer to Luke."

"No you don't have to, but the way he looks at you, I think he's on the hook."

"On the hook?"

"Ally, he cares about you and what happens to you. That's not something you want to take for granted."

"Maybe not, but right now, I'm more concerned with staying out of jail, and hopefully getting Denise out of jail, too." The elevator doors slid open. Ally stepped out into an empty hallway. Charlotte followed after her. Ally watched for any doors that might swing open as she walked. She didn't want to be surprised by the sudden appearance of someone. When she reached the door she took out the gloves from her pocket and put them on, then she took the key from her grandmother and slid it into the door. When the door opened Ally sighed with relief and stepped inside.

"I'll stay out here in case I see anyone coming. You can tell me what you see."

Ally looked over the room. It was identical to the one she had stayed in, aside from the bed being stripped and the drawers hanging open. The police had done a thorough search. But they might have overlooked something. Ally looked at the table where she assumed the wine glasses would have been. She looked under the mattress, in the bottom of the closet. She even checked under the sink in the small bathroom. There wasn't a trace of any evidence. She grimaced as she wondered whether all of this had been for nothing.

She walked back into the bedroom. She knelt down and took one more look around. Something on the floor hidden in the small gap under the bed caught her eye. It was glimmering. She bent down and held her breath. She looked closer and saw that it was a small diamond earring. She didn't want to touch it in case it was evidence so she pulled out her phone and took a photo of it. She put her phone into her pocket and slowly stood up. If she could figure out who wore the earring she might be able to figure out who the murderer was or at least who had drinks with Dustin. It appeared that drinks might have turned into something more. Which again pointed at Denise, as they might have rekindled their relationship. Ally turned to step out of the room and heard her grandmother's voice in the hallway.

"Oh, I'm sorry. I must be at the wrong door. This is a crime scene? I had no idea. But could you help me find my room? At my age I get a little confused, you know. Would you please?"

Ally held her breath as she looked for a place to hide.

"Sorry ma'am, I don't have time right now. I'm sure if you go down to the lobby and ask for help they will help you."

"Sure. But that's so far. I'm sure that you could..."

"Ma'am, I could call down to the lobby to have someone come up if you like, but I am going to need you to clear the area while I secure the room."

Ally closed her eyes. There was nowhere to hide. The closet was too small. The bed was too close to the ground to hide underneath it. Even if she could get out the window, it was too high up to risk it. She did the only thing she could think of, she went into the bathroom and stepped into the bathtub. She pulled the curtain closed. A moment later she heard the door open. Her heart pounded. This was it. She was going to be caught returning to the scene of the crime. How would that look to a jury? How would it look to Luke, who expected her to be at the cottage? She gritted her teeth and tried to think of a good excuse for when she got caught. Just as she planned out a good insanity defense, a loud siren began to ring through the room. Her eyes widened. It was a fire alarm.

"Oh seriously? I just started!" The man in the room groaned. She heard him walk to the door. Then she heard the door close behind him. Ally was sure that Charlotte must have been the one to pull the fire alarm. She hurried out into the room. She opened the door just a crack and peeked out into the hall. People emptied their rooms and filled the corridor as they shuffled towards the stairwell. Ally stepped out and blended right in with them. She noticed a woman come out from the room across the hall. She looked at Ally. Ally looked back at her. The exchange felt tense, but Ally had no idea why. Did the woman see Ally step out of the crime scene? Ally turned and hurried down the hall. Charlotte greeted her in the lobby.

"Did you do what I think you did?" Ally raised an eyebrow.

"Never mind that. What had to be done, was done. Now let's get out of here, fast."

"Yes, let's..." Ally glanced back over her shoulder once, and noticed Ben in the middle of the lobby. He looked in her direction, but appeared to look past her at the group of people that exited the hotel. Ally tried not to worry as she and her grandmother walked around to the back of the hotel.

"Did you find anything in the room?"

"Yes, actually I did. I'm not sure that it will mean anything, but I found a diamond earring under the bed. It could have been there from another guest, but it could also be from whoever had a glass of wine with Dustin."

"It's a good start. What did you do with it?"

"I left it there and took a photo of it with my phone."

"Good thinking, if you took it, it couldn't be used as evidence."

"That's what I thought. I just hope it doesn't go missing before the murderer is caught."

"Good point."

Ally's phone began to ring. She was almost to the parking lot of the grocery store when she checked to see who it was. Her heart lurched when she saw that it was Luke.

"Hello?"

"Where are you?"

"Uh." Ally glanced at her grandmother. "Out, for a walk."

"Then you should be able to get right back to the cottage?"

"Uh." She opened the door to the van. "I think it might be a few minutes."

"Where are you?" Luke repeated.

"Why? Is something wrong?"

"Detective Ballantine is at the cottage right now. He said you weren't there. He's not too happy. I thought you said you were going to stay put?"

"What does the detective want?"

Charlotte started the van.

"Ally, are you in a car? Where did you go?" He sighed. "You know what, don't tell me. Just get back to the cottage as soon as possible." He hung up the phone before Ally had a chance to respond. She winced as her grandmother pulled out of the parking lot.

"Ballantine is waiting for me at the cottage."

"Did Luke say why?"

"No. I'm sure he wouldn't tell me to go back if he thought it was to get arrested though. Well, at least he wouldn't have at the beginning of the phone call. Now, I'm not so sure."

"He's upset?"

Ally stared out through the windshield. "Very."

"Well, maybe he'll brighten up when he finds out that we have a photo of the earring."

"Maybe." Ally bit into her bottom lip. "But I don't exactly want to have to tell him we were in the room."

The closer Ally got to Blue River the more anxious she became. What if Ballantine was there to arrest her? Sure the case had been handed over to the Mainbry police department, but that didn't mean that Ballantine couldn't come up with another reason to arrest her or arrest her on their behalf.

Chapter Seven

As the van approached the cottage Ally saw that Ballantine stood in front of it.

"Want me to keep driving?" Charlotte glanced over at her.

"No. That might get Luke in trouble. I need to at least cooperate for his sake. I mean he has been defending me."

"All right." She reached out and gave Ally's hand a squeeze. "We're in this together, okay?"

Ally nodded. Charlotte parked the van in the driveway. Ally stepped out and walked towards the detective very slowly.

"Well, you're a bit hard to find, Ally Sweet." He put his hands on his hips which made his belly look even rounder. "Where have you been?"

"Is there something I can help you with, Detective?"

"Absolutely. I'd like to know why you were helping your friend Denise hide Dustin's body."

"I wasn't." Ally crossed her arms. "Denise did not do this."

"You know that how?'

"I know that because she's a good person who would never hurt anyone, just like me," Ally said firmly. "I'm sorry, Detective, but you have this all wrong."

"You might think that right now, but you're going to find out things are very different once she's in front of a jury. I'm sorry, Ally, but there's nothing about this case that makes Denise or you look innocent, including the fact that your boyfriend met you at the carwash, in his patrol car."

"He's not my boyfriend." Ally set her jaw. "Now, you're just trying to upset me. I know what you're doing. You can spin this however you want, but neither of us had any idea that Dustin was in my trunk when I stopped at the carwash."

"Then why is it that you decided to wash your car right after staying at the hotel?"

Charlotte walked up behind Ally, but remained silent.

"To be honest it was because of the valet. When he drove the car back to me I was pretty embarrassed that it was so dirty. I probably wouldn't have noticed otherwise. So I decided since I had some extra time I would hit the carwash on the way home."

"Pretty convenient."

"If you say so. However, I had no idea at that point that anything was in my trunk."

"I also noticed that your trunk was pretty much empty. To make room for a body?"

"No, to make room for the boxes I intended to move to my grandmother's apartment at Freely Lakes. I've been through all of this before. I thought Mainbry was assigned to the case now?"

"Mainbry is. I'm helping out, since you're a local."

"How generous of you."

"I like to think so. Ah, Elm, I didn't think it would be long before you showed up."

Ally turned to see Luke walk up the driveway. He scowled as he looked at Ballantine.

"Why are you questioning her without her lawyer?"

"She didn't ask for a lawyer. Did you?"

Ballantine looked at Ally.

"No I didn't."

Luke looked over at her, then back at Ballantine. "What is this about?"

"Mainbry police took Denise Mitchell into custody. So far she's not talking. So, I thought maybe Ally would give me some idea of how she knows Denise."

"Do you really want to know?" Ally sighed.

"You don't have to tell him anything, Ally." Luke frowned.

"Who exactly do you work for again, Elm?"

"I know her rights," Luke said.

"Stop." Ally held up her hand. "It's fine. I'll tell him. Denise was good friends with my mother, before she passed away. She moved away so I haven't seen her for years."

"I'm sorry for your loss, Ally, but all that tells me is that you don't know Denise very well at all," Detective Ballantine said.

"No, I guess I don't. But my grandmother is friends with her mother. Isn't that right, Mee-Maw?"

"Yes, I am. I know Denise quite well, and she would never hurt anyone." Charlotte folded her hands in front of her. "Maybe you'd like to add me as a suspect to your list?"

Ballantine smirked at her. "A beautiful woman such as yourself? I doubt that you'd step on an ant."

Charlotte glared at him as he turned his attention back to Ally. "So, the two main suspects in a murder case would never hurt anyone. But someone is dead."

"And you're wasting your time here, when you could be investigating the actual crime," Luke said.

"Watch it, Elm," Ballantine warned. "I've already spoken to the chief about how close you are to this case. Don't make me file a complaint on top of it."

"Luke isn't doing anything wrong." Ally felt her cheeks heat up as she tried to control her anger at Ballantine's accusation and rudeness.

"Maybe not to you," Ballantine said.

"Enough." Luke stepped away from Ally and

came to Ballantine's side. "We're on the same side, whether you realize it or not. If I suspected that Ally had anything to do with this crime, I would be doing the same thing that you are. But I know that she doesn't. Yes, I am willing to stake my badge on it, so don't bother with the threats. If you really want to be of help, you should try finding out who stole the surveillance video from the hotel."

"There are people working on that."

"One more couldn't hurt." Luke straightened his shoulders. "It will certainly get you a lot further than standing here."

"You better not be wrong about Ally, Elm. Or you're going to lose more than your badge." Ballantine turned and walked away. Charlotte unlocked the front door. Ally pulled Luke into the cottage.

"You have to stop that."

"Stop what?" Luke asked.

"Stop risking things for me." Ally crossed her arms and looked into his eyes.

"I'll just give you two some privacy." Charlotte

stepped into the kitchen.

"Ally, I'm not going to apologize for that."

"Why not? Don't you know how terrible it makes me feel every time you risk your career for me?"

"I'm sorry that you feel that way, but I'm not sorry for taking the risk. I believe that you are innocent."

"Luke..."

He stepped in front of her and looked into her eyes again. "I'm going to help you."

"You're quite stubborn, you know that?"

"I have to be. You're more stubborn than me."

Ally laughed. "You always make me smile, even when I'm ready to scream."

"So, what did you find?"

"What do you mean?"

"Ally, I know you went to the hotel to search for something or to talk to someone. So, what did you find?"

"You're not mad?"

"What would be the point?" He smiled at her. "It doesn't seem to matter to you if I think you're making the right choice."

"That's not exactly true."

"It doesn't matter right now. What matters right now is whether we can find some evidence to clear your name. So, what did you find?"

"I found a diamond earring."

"Where?" He watched as she pulled her phone out of her pocket.

"Under the bed in the room that Dustin stayed in."

"Ally! You broke into the crime scene? I knew you had something to do with that false fire alarm at the hotel, I just knew it."

"Actually, that was me." Charlotte raised her hand as she walked back into the living room.

"The two of you." Luke rolled his eyes to the ceiling, then looked at the photo of the earring that Ally showed him.

"If we can find the matching one, then we might find out who shared wine with Dustin or even who the murderer is," Ally said.

"That's true, but how are we going to find it? It's not like a diamond stud is that unusual. The person who lost it might not even miss it," Luke said as he took her phone from her and looked at the photo. "And now of course I somehow have to get Mainbry to go back and search the room without letting them know that I know it's there."

"We won't have to tell them if we find the person it belongs to and we get a confession or admission out of them," Ally said.

"We first have to find them, which is the hard part," Luke said.

"If the person does know that it's missing, I bet she's pretty interested in getting it back," Ally said. "She will probably try to get back into the room."

"Maybe. But, if she doesn't know it's missing in the room she might think that she lost it somewhere else," Luke said.

"Well, at the very least we know that it's a woman who can afford to wear a diamond stud earring. That might help us figure out who it is." Charlotte shrugged. "Or eliminate who it isn't."

"That's true. But maybe it has nothing to do with Dustin at all. Maybe it's from a previous guest," Ally said.

"It's possible. I found out that the lead homicide detective from Mainbry is pretty frustrated with the response he got from the staff at the hotel. I guess because Denise has been arrested. I think they feel they want to protect her."

"That doesn't surprise me. Denise is a likeable person."

"Apparently Denise and Dustin were engaged at one point."

"That still doesn't mean that she did anything to him," Ally said defensively.

"Of course it doesn't, but it lends credence to the idea that they might have gotten into a lover's spat." He sighed. "I can't question the staff and without video surveillance we're really playing a guessing game."

"I think the next step is to talk to Denise." Ally looked over at Luke. "She is the key to getting more information."

"She's still in custody." Luke shook his head. "I don't know if we can make that happen."

"Isn't she allowed visitors?" Ally asked.

"Yes Ally, but you have to be cautious. You don't want to make yourself look more guilty by going to visit. We need to figure out a way to prevent that."

"I'm not sure if there is one. I'm just going to visit a friend. I can't waste my time worrying about what people think. I think that Ballantine thinks I'm guilty, and who knows what he is telling the Mainbry detectives. I think it's important that we find out the truth as soon as possible." She braced herself for an argument from Luke, but he only nodded.

"I think you're right, Ally. The best way to find out what has happened is to talk to her." He met her eyes for a lingering moment. Ally was the first one to look away.

"Can I go now?" She asked hopefully.

"No, you'll have to wait until tomorrow. It's too late now, and she's probably not processed yet."

"I feel awful every time I think of her being stuck in there," Ally said.

"It's not your fault that she's there, Ally." Charlotte hugged her.

"Isn't it? If I had just looked in my trunk, maybe all of this could have been solved faster. As it is some evidence might have been destroyed because I took the car through the carwash. There might have been prints, or something that the police could have used to identify the killer."

"I doubt that if someone went to all the trouble of putting the body in the trunk, that they didn't bother to wear gloves or be careful not to leave a print. I think what you need is a night of rest, Ally," Luke said. "I'll try and set up a time for you to see Denise in the morning. I'll stop by on my way to work and let you know if I managed to arrange it."

"Thanks Luke." Ally looked into his eyes.

"Make sure you get some rest, you look tired."

"I'll try."

"Do you want to stay for dinner, Luke? I can fix something real quick." Charlotte started back into the kitchen.

"No thanks. I'm meeting someone actually."

Those words made Ally's head snap back towards him. "Oh?" Ally said.

"Yes. In fact I should leave now or I'm going to be late. Call me if you need anything, Ally." He turned and walked out of the cottage. Ally stared after him in mild shock.

"Ally?" Charlotte asked.

"Why did you invite him to dinner?" Ally looked at her grandmother.

"I thought it might be nice."

"Well, clearly he is not interested." Ally shook her head.

"Someone sounds jealous. Maybe if you showed more interest in him, you wouldn't have to be worried about who he's having dinner with. Come help me make some pasta."

"I don't know if I can eat."

"Trust me, when you smell my sauce you'll be able to eat."

"I hope so." Ally rubbed her stomach. "It's been a long day."

Ally joined her grandmother at the stove to help her make the sauce. Really it was just a way to distract herself from what had happened. She didn't want to think about the possibility of being arrested, or Denise not getting out. She just wanted to be with her grandmother, relaxed and laughing over splattered sauce. However, once dinner was on the table it was clear that Charlotte had other intentions.

"So, about Luke."

"No, I don't want to talk about him."

"Ally."

"Mee-Maw." She took a big bite of her pasta so that she wouldn't be able to talk for some time.

"Sweetheart, I know that you got your heart broken." She patted Ally's hand. "But you have to know a good man when you see one."

"I do. I know that Luke is a good man. But that doesn't make him the man for me."

"He's quite insistent that he is."

"Mee-Maw, he's just flirting."

"You can tell yourself that, but I think you know better, Ally." Charlotte passed her a roll and buttered her own to go with her pasta. "If you keep pushing him away, he's going to have more dinners with other people. Are you going to be able to handle that?"

Ally set her jaw. She wanted to argue with her grandmother, but she couldn't. She had hit the nail on the head. Maybe Ally wasn't ready for dating Luke, but she didn't relish the idea of Luke dating anyone else.

"Maybe not." Ally finished her food and picked up her plate. "But what I do know is that until this case is solved, I can't even think about it." She took her grandmother's plate. "I'll handle the dishes."

"Are you sure?"

"Absolutely. You're the guest, remember?"

"Ha!" Charlotte tossed a dish towel at her. "Better watch that sass, young lady, I will never be a guest in this house."

Ally smiled as she caught the towel. "That's very true."

"I think I'll go home and check on Rose. If she has heard the news she will be very upset."

"Okay. Is it okay if I drop you off and then I can keep the van to go to Denise in the morning?"

"You can have the van. I want to walk home though."

"Are you sure?"

"Yes, it's still light out and I could use a little exercise."

"As long as you're sure, Mee-Maw, you know I don't mind taking you."

"Of course I know that." Charlotte smiled. "Do you want me to come with you to Denise tomorrow?"

"No thanks, I'll be fine. It's better if you open the shop."

"Okay. Ally, when you see Denise, please tell her that I'm thinking of her."

"I will." She hugged her grandmother and walked her to the door. Arnold came to the door to say goodbye. Charlotte bent down and pet the pig on the head.

Once Ally had watched her grandmother walk down the driveway, she returned to the kitchen. As she washed the dishes she went back through the events of the day. If there was just one thing that she missed, she might never be able to solve the case. However, even going back through it in her mind didn't yield any results. She finished the last dish and put it in the drainer. She leaned against the counter for a moment. The weight of the day was heavy on her shoulders.

Even though it had only been a few hours since they had found Dustin, it seemed like a lifetime. Ally wondered what Denise was doing at the same moment. She recalled her mother and Denise laughing and playing cards at the kitchen table, while she did her best to play along. Denise was a big part of her childhood, and she didn't want to fail her. She walked away from the counter and into her room. Peaches followed right after her. When she sat down on her bed, Peaches jumped right up into her lap.

"Yes, I need to talk." Ally pet the top of the cat's head. "I just don't understand how the body ended up in my trunk. It could have been the valet, he has access to all the keys. But I'm sure there are other people at the hotel that have access to those things, too. The valet can't be the only suspect." She flopped back against the bed and yawned. "Luke was right, I am exhausted."

Peaches bumped her head against her cheek and meowed. "Oh no, we're not talking about Luke." Peaches meowed again. Ally looked into her eyes. "I'm just not ready, Peaches. I'm not sure I ever will be." She sighed and snuggled the cat close. Through all the rough nights she had with her ex-husband Peaches had been there for emotional support. Ally treasured her.

As Ally fell asleep she considered whether she was ready to go out with Luke. But the quick fear that rose within her, warned her that she was not. "Maybe I'm meant to be alone for a little while, Peaches. What's so wrong with that?" Peaches purred and nuzzled her chin. "I know, I know. I'm never alone. I have you." Ally smiled as she drifted off to sleep.

Chapter Eight

When Ally woke the next morning she hurried to feed the animals. Then she prepared a fresh pot of coffee. She cut two bagels and set out butter and cream cheese. Once the table was set, she checked her phone. It was almost nine and still no text from Luke. She started to wonder if he had forgotten. After another ten minutes slid by, Ally was very antsy. She decided to call him and see what he was up to and if he had managed to make a time. She dialed his number. After several rings she was about to hang up. Then he picked up. At least, she thought he did.

"Hi Luke?" She heard noise in the background. "Luke, are you there?"

"Listen, we've talked about this before. I still can't believe you left without telling me. But I know we need to work through this."

A garbled voice responded to him, she couldn't make out what it was saying. Ally realized that the answer button had inadvertently been pressed. It had happened to her on a few occasions when her phone was in her pocket on silent.

Ally's heart sunk. It certainly sounded like he was trying to make up with someone. A past lover? She tensed at the thought. No matter who it was, she was obviously more important than coming to Ally as arranged. She hung up the phone and tried not to get upset. She didn't have a right to be, after all. She didn't know what to do. She had no idea if the meeting had been arranged at the prison. She decided that she would wait a little longer and hopefully Luke would call her. Otherwise she would go to Mainbry prison and try and see Denise. She ate her bagel and then started to clean up the rest of the breakfast that she had set out. Just as she picked up the plate with Luke's bagel on it there was a knock on the door. When she answered it, Luke was on the other side.

"Oh. Hi." Ally did her best to avoid his eyes.

"Sorry, I'm running late. Is that coffee I smell?"

"Well, I missed breakfast yesterday, and I thought you might want to have breakfast together today."

"Wow, thanks Ally."

"Sure. Let me just toast this for you."

"Thanks." Luke smiled as she walked over to the toaster.

"Here." She offered him the toasted bagel, and again avoided his eyes.

"Thanks. Are you okay?" He tipped his head to the side in an attempt to meet her eyes.

"I'm fine."

"I managed to set up a meeting with you and Denise."

"Thanks!" Ally sighed with relief.

"Sorry I can't come with you."

"That's okay." She smiled but continued to avoid eye contact. "I'll be fine. I appreciate what you've done for me already."

"It's no problem. You'll have to leave soon though," he said. "The appointment is at ten."

"Why don't we take these on the road?"

"A mobile breakfast?"

"I'm just anxious to see Denise."

"All right, if that's what you want that's fine. I

appreciate the breakfast, sorry I was late for it."

"It's okay. We didn't set a time really. I know you're busy, Luke."

"Never too busy for you."

"Sure." She forced a smile and poured their coffee into travel mugs. On the way out the door she gave Peaches a scratch under her chin.

"Let me know how you go with seeing Denise." He looked at her as they got to the van.

"I will."

"Call me if you need anything." He opened up the van door for her.

"Thank you for helping me, Luke."

"You're welcome." He looked at her. "I'll always be here for you, Ally."

Ally smiled to herself. She wanted to argue the point, to remind him that she was just fine on her own, but she knew that he wouldn't listen. She was glad that he wouldn't.

As Ally drove to Mainbry she was anxious. Not just about seeing Denise, but about Luke as well. No matter how many times she told herself that she didn't have a reason to be upset about what she had overheard, she couldn't deny a dull ache in the pit of her stomach. She'd misread Luke completely. His playful flirting really was just playful flirting. What she had overheard on the phone was the truth. He cared about someone very deeply.

Ally was surprised as she turned into the prison parking lot. She had been so distracted she had driven on autopilot. At the gate she leaned through the window and told the guard her details. The guard checked the details and waved her through.

Things are much easier when you go through the front door, she thought to herself. She parked near the building and got out of the van. She walked quickly towards the entrance and walked over to security and went through the various procedures. Although there were many the process was surprisingly quick. Once she was through security Ally felt more confident. This would be her chance to find out information from Denise that could solve the murder. She couldn't be distracted by Luke's phone call.

When Ally walked into the visitor's room, Denise was already seated at the table. Her hands were cuffed, but she was otherwise free. Ally sat down in the chair on the other side of the table. It was hard to look at Denise when she was so upset, but she knew she had to. Denise's eyes were puffy and she barely looked at Ally.

"Why did you come here?" She sniffled.

"Because I want to help you, Denise."

"What can you do?" She shook her head. "They've made up their minds. I don't know why, but they think I did this. They think I put him in your car, so that you would help me. Ally, how did he get there?"

"I don't know, Denise. That's what I'm trying to figure out. Did you and Dustin get together that night? Did you have wine?"

"No." She sighed. "Not that it matters. No one believes me. We were supposed to get together, but not for romance. He said he wanted to tell me something about one of the staff members. Something he found out. I went by his room after my shift, but he didn't answer the door. I figured he got caught up in something, and that he would tell me whatever he needed to tell me today. I just went home, alone. Which apparently isn't a solid alibi."

"No, it's not." Ally grimaced. "What about Dustin? Was he seeing anyone? Did you notice him flirting with anyone? Someone was in that room with him and shared a glass of wine."

"I don't know. We didn't really talk about things like that. He didn't mention anyone. He was a bit of a flirt with everybody. I even warned him about it earlier that day. There was a guest checking in, and he started flirting pretty heavily. When she turned him down, I took him aside. I warned him that he couldn't do that type of thing at the hotel."

"Did you tell the police that?"

"No, I'm not telling them anything. Everything I've told them they turned against me."

"Do you remember the name of the guest?" Ally leaned forward.

"No, I don't know who she was. Just some

cute blonde. It wasn't like I was jealous or anything, I just didn't want him to get fired."

"I understand. What about anyone else in his life? Did he ever mention anyone that might have been a problem when you were together?"

"Not that I know about. He spent all of his time working, or with me, and then when we ended things, I don't know what he did. I've never even seen him get frustrated, let alone angry at someone." She lowered her eyes. "He was a good man. He didn't deserve this."

"You don't deserve it either, Denise. I promise, I'm trying to find the real murderer."

"Thank you, Ally. But please, don't put yourself in a dangerous situation. Your mother, she wouldn't want that."

Ally longed to reach across the table and touch her hand, but she didn't know if that was allowed. "No she wouldn't. But she wouldn't want you in here either."

"Just be careful. They keep asking me questions about you. I'm worried that they might think we worked together."

"It's going to be okay, Denise, I'm going to get you out of here. Just hang on a little longer for me."

"I don't really want you involved in all of this, Ally, but there's one person at the hotel that I know would want to help me. Talk to Kylie, we worked together before. She's the assistant manager and usually works in reception. She'll be able to get to things that no one else can."

"Okay, I will. What about the staff member that he wanted to talk to you about? Do you have any idea who it was?"

"No." She shook her head. "He wouldn't tell me anything over the phone. He seemed a little upset by it. But he didn't say why." She reached up and wiped away a tear. "Maybe if I had gone to his room earlier, or made him meet me somewhere. I don't know. I still can't believe he's gone."

"I'm sorry, Denise, I know this is a lot for you to deal with. Just try to hang in there. I'm working on it. Okay?"

She smiled a little as she nodded. "Thanks Ally."

"Denise. You're not missing any earrings are you?"

"Not that I know of." She shook her head. "Why?"

"Oh nothing." Ally shrugged. "I'll be in touch soon."

As Ally walked out of the room an urge to bring Denise with her flooded through her body. Were it not for the armed guard that escorted her to the front lobby, she might have tried to. When Ally got outside she walked quickly to the van. She called Luke to let him know how it went.

"Hi Ally," Luke answered quickly.

"I managed to see Denise?"

"Oh good," Luke said. "How did it go?"

"She didn't know much. Just that Dustin wanted to speak to her last night about a staff member, but she never caught up with him."

"Does Denise know who?"

"No, but she did give me the name of someone who might be able to help with getting more information. The assistant manager, Kylie."

"I'm sure that she has already been

questioned quite a bit."

"I'm sure she has, too, but if she and Denise are good friends, she might not have told the police everything that she would tell me. I'd like to see if she has anything more to say. Plus, she might have an idea who the earring belongs to."

"That earring could be a dead end. It's a pretty common style and it doesn't prove anything."

"Maybe. But it's just about all we have right now."

"While you were in with Denise, I had an update on the case. It turns out all of the surveillance video from the hotel has been damaged or deleted."

"All of it?" Ally raised an eyebrow. "That's not disabling cameras then, someone got inside the security office."

"Yes, it seems that way. The more I learn about this case the stranger it gets. Someone went to a whole lot of trouble to kill Dustin and cover their tracks."

"I bet it has something to do with what he found out about a member of staff. If only he'd told Denise who it was, we'd have our prime suspect, I know it."

"As of right now Denise is the main suspect. You should be grateful for that, because if it wasn't for her they'd probably be going after you." Luke grimaced. "Sorry, I shouldn't have pointed that out."

"It's okay. It's the truth. But it doesn't make me feel any better about Denise being in there. We have to find a way to get her out, as soon as possible."

"I have to get back to work, but if you need me you can call me anytime, all right?"

"Yes, I appreciate that."

"Just lay low and don't do any investigating. Please."

"Don't worry."

"I'll check in with you as soon as I hear anything new."

"Thanks." Ally smiled. "Thank you for your support."

"Anytime." He hung up the phone.

Ally started the van and drove to the shop. As

she got out of the van she turned towards the shop in time to see the door swing open.

"Ally, I'm glad that you're back." Charlotte stepped outside to meet her. "How is she?"

Ally hugged her grandmother. "Not great, not where she is. I am more determined than ever to help her. I need to find out who the murderer is and clear her name. I just hope that I actually can."

"If anyone can I know it's you, Ally. You have the mind for it. What's the next step?" Charlotte guided her inside the shop.

"I think we need to get as much information as we can. The best way to do that is to talk to as many people at the hotel as we can. Someone had to have seen something, or know something. Denise gave me the name of someone who will be able to help us. The assistant manager, Kylie."

"Oh good, that will give us a place to start. In my experience though, people are always much more talkative if they are bribed."

"I don't think we have the kind of cash that we would need for bribery."

"Maybe not cash, but we do have something that might be even better."

"What's that?" Ally lifted an eyebrow.

"Chocolate. I've got some spare, and we can make a few more batches to take with us. If we are handing out the chocolates we will have an excuse for being there, too."

"That is a great idea. How has everything been at the shop? In all of this I feel like I'm neglecting it."

"Don't worry about that. I've been taking care of things."

"I know. Thank you, Mee-Maw." She sighed and looked into her eyes. "You're so patient with me, Mee-Maw."

"Ally, don't you know how much it means to me that I can rely on you to handle the shop?"

"I just hope I'm doing it well enough. You worked so hard to build up the reputation, I don't want to do anything to change that."

"Let me stop you right there, because you will change it, sweetheart. You are going to put your own style and touches on it. That is what I want more than anything. The business was never supposed to be just mine, it was supposed to be something our family could share. I don't want you to worry, I want you to embrace it and make it your own."

"Thank you, Mee-Maw." Ally hugged her again. "I can't wait to make some more chocolates with you."

Chapter Nine

When Ally and Charlotte went back into the shop Ally felt a sense of relief. She did her best thinking while creating chocolate. With a little music to keep them in the creative mood they began to work together on an assembly line of chocolates. Ally thought about the many times she had done this with her grandmother and her own mother.

With Denise back in Ally's life, it was hard not to think about the special memories she had of her mother. Although it had been many years since Ally had said goodbye to her, she still had moments when it felt as fresh as the day it happened. Her heart ached for her mother in a way that she knew would always be with her. But every time she felt that ache she also felt incredibly lucky to have her grandmother in her life. When the chocolates were ready they packaged each one.

"It might bring back bad memories for the

staff if we take the caramel chocolates to the hotel if they know they might have been the last thing Dustin ate. We can leave them here because the ladies didn't get to try any yet. I bet Mrs. Bing is going to love them."

"Good thinking, Ally. I really think the new recipe is going to be a hit."

After closing the shop they loaded all of the samples into the van and headed off to Mainbry. Ally drove the route that was becoming very familiar. She wondered if there would be a time when she could look at the big blue hotel as just a building, and not a crime scene. It was a shame that something so tragic had happened when the hotel had only been open for such a short period of time.

When they reached Mainbry Charlotte nervously looked over her shoulder at the pile of boxes.

"Are you sure we have enough samples?"

"Don't worry, we have plenty." Ally pushed the switch for what she thought was the turn signal, but instead turned on the windshield wipers. She groaned and turned on the correct switch. "I really appreciate you letting me use the van, Mee-Maw, but I am looking forward to getting my car back."

"You don't want a new one?" Charlotte raised an eyebrow as she looked over at her.

"No, I don't think so. I'll have it cleaned inside and out of course, but it's still my car."

"You're so down to earth, Ally. Someone else might never get in that car again."

"I have too many good memories in it."

"I understand," Charlotte said.

Ally pulled through the circular driveway of the hotel. Before she could drive past, the valet stepped down off the curb. He smiled at her through the open window.

"Welcome. Can I have your keys please?" He reached his hand out to her.

"Actually, I'd like to park it myself."

"Uh, that's very unusual."

"Do you recognize me?" She leaned out the window some so that he could see her.

"Yes." His eyes widened.

"Last time I let you take my car, it came back with a body in it. So, you'll understand if I'd like to park the van myself. Just tell me where the parking lot is, and I will park it." She met his eyes. "I have a delivery of chocolates."

"Oh, if you have a delivery that's okay," he said quickly. "It's down the drive and to the right."

"Thank you," Ally said as she started to drive off.

"Ally? What are you doing?" Charlotte asked. "I doubt that we'll find another dead body if we leave the van with the valet."

"Probably not, but this way we can see where the car was parked." She noticed the parking lot entrance off to the right of the hotel. She drove down the driveway to the parking lot which was in the basement of the hotel. There were several cars parked in it. She took the next empty slot. When she parked she looked over the surroundings of the parking lot. There were a few doors that faced the parking lot, and what looked like a chute.

"What do you think this is?" Ally walked up to it and rapped on the side with her knuckles.

Charlotte narrowed her eyes. She leaned close to the opening.

"I think it's a laundry chute. They probably send out their bedding and towels to a service. The truck pulls up here and it gets loaded through the chute," Charlotte said.

Ally tilted her head and peered up inside the chute. "It looks pretty big."

"Big enough for a body?" Charlotte asked.

"It would explain how he got into my trunk and why he was wrapped in Denise's jacket. Whoever did it could have backed the car right up to the chute. Terrible."

"Yes, but I think you're right. If this was how Dustin's body was moved then we know that whoever did it, had access to the laundry, and the valet keys. I think we're definitely looking at an inside job here."

"We'd better get inside before the valet notices us looking around. Who knows who is involved?" Ally gritted her teeth. "Anyone could be watching."

Charlotte shivered and nodded. Ally held the

door for her grandmother. Once Charlotte was inside Ally stepped in behind her. Guests dotted the lobby. Ally noticed Kylie at the front desk. As she walked towards the front desk she also noticed that there were a few people watching her. The staff had likely been informed of her potential involvement. Luckily, right beside her, Charlotte carried the boxes of chocolates.

"Good morning." Ally smiled.

"Good morning." Kylie nodded at her. Ally took note of the heavy circles under her eyes. If she had to guess, she would say that Kylie hadn't slept at all the night before. In fact, she had likely been crying.

"I've been to see Denise this morning," Ally said.

Charlotte set the boxes of samples on the counter. She opened the box on top. "We brought chocolates!"

"Wait, what?" Kylie met Ally's eyes. "You went to see Denise in jail?"

"Yes. I wanted to get her side of things."

"Oh." Kylie frowned. "Is she okay?"

"She is, for now. But we're going to have to move fast if we want to help her." Ally pushed the box towards her. "I need to talk to the staff. Kitchen, valet, laundry, maids, anyone who was here when Dustin was killed."

"I don't know." Kylie glanced around the lobby. "Ben has been on a rampage. I don't think he would be too happy about the two of you wandering through here."

"Denise told me that you and her are friends and you would try to help me clear her name. Is that true?" Ally raised an eyebrow and studied the woman's face. Kylie lowered her eyes.

"It's true. I know that Denise didn't do this. Dustin was a good man, he didn't deserve this. I just don't know how I can help."

"You can help by giving us access and introducing us to a few of the staff so we can ask some questions." Charlotte leaned across the desk some. "Denise is very important to me, and I want her home safe as soon as possible."

"I want the same thing. I guess we can find a way to make this work," Kylie said.

"The focus is off me right now," Ally said. "I think with Denise in custody, the detective on the case is satisfied. If Ben asks what we're doing here, you can tell him that we're distributing more samples. As far as I am concerned we are still trying to convince him to order the chocolates for the hotel. Does that sound okay to you?"

"Yes, that sounds perfect. He hasn't said anything about not going with your shop. Still, it's important to keep in mind that rumors have been flying around the hotel, some of the staff may not be so willing to talk. Where do you want to start?"

Ally straightened up. "In the kitchen. I want to figure out who had drinks with Dustin before he died. Denise said that it wasn't her, and I believe her. I already know that Dustin didn't order the wine, so we need to pin down who brought that wine into his room. They were hotel wine glasses, so the wine had to be ordered from the kitchen."

"Yes, that's right. I'll call the chef and try to convince him to let the staff talk to you and I'll do my best to keep Ben away from the kitchen. But I can't risk losing my job, not even to protect Denise. Okay?" She met Ally's eyes.

"I understand. We'll be careful."

Ally and Charlotte took one of the boxes of chocolates and headed down the side hall towards the kitchen.

"I hope the staff don't recognize me from when I acted as a diversion," Charlotte said. "If they do I'll just have to do a little more acting." She smiled.

The smell of freshly chopped onions greeted Ally as she stepped into the kitchen. Charlotte followed right behind her. A few of the staff members turned to look at Ally.

As they walked in a man with a thick chest and thick brown hair under his chef's hat eyed Ally.

"We brought samples." Charlotte displayed the assortment of chocolates in the box. "Want to try some?" The moment he saw the chocolates his entire demeanor changed. The staff didn't seem to recognize Charlotte from the indigestion incident.

"Sure." He grinned.

As he and the others enjoyed their chocolates

Ally decided it was time to ask him some questions.

"I have a couple of questions if you don't mind." Ally smiled.

"Okay, Kylie said you might have a few. I will do what I can to help. I like Denise," he said.

"Thank you," Ally said. "How many guests order wine on an average night?"

"Oh, I'd say at least fifty percent of the guests. It's complimentary with the room, so most don't pass up the opportunity."

Ally cringed. If there were that many glasses of wine delivered to that many rooms then how would she narrow down who brought the wine into Dustin's room?

"Hm. I don't know about everyone else, Ally, but I know that I wouldn't be able to carry two glasses of wine very far without spilling," Charlotte said. "I would think whoever ordered the wine and brought it into Dustin's room had to be someone with a room near his. At least on the same floor."

"You're right!" Ally snapped her fingers and

then looked back at the chef. "Can you get us a list of all of the rooms that ordered wine on Dustin's floor?"

"Sure I can. Will that help?"

"It's a start." Ally nodded. "Thank you."

"Will you leave some of those samples?" He offered a half-smile.

"Plenty." Charlotte began piling some up on a plate for the staff while the head chef looked through the orders.

"It looks like ten people ordered wine on that floor. That's actually not as many as I expected."

"Anyone close to Dustin's room?" Ally peered over his shoulder at the list.

"Yes, the guest across from him, Brenna, ordered two glasses." He paused a moment. "Actually, that's a little odd, as she checked in alone. Of course she might have had company." He shrugged.

"That's perfect! Thank you. Can I have a copy of that list?"

"I don't feel comfortable with that," he said apologetically. "But I can give you the details for the room across from Dustin's."

"Thanks, that's great," Ally said. She really wanted the whole list but she didn't want to push her luck.

"Do you think it was her?" Charlotte closed up the box of samples as the chef went to copy the details.

"I remember seeing her when I left Dustin's room because of the fire alarm. She did seem a bit off. But then again, finding out that the room across from yours is a crime scene can do that to anyone. I want to head straight for her room and see if we can get some information from her before she decides to check out."

"Here are the details." The chef handed Ally a piece of paper.

"Thanks." Ally took it from him and started to leave the kitchen. She paused at the door and turned back. "What do you do with your soiled towels and things?"

"Oh, we have a door to the chute." He pointed to a square on the wall.

"Won't it fall out into the parking lot?"

Charlotte asked.

"There's a small compartment that we fill up. When the truck arrives we pull the lever and it goes out through the chute."

"Are there any other doors to the chute?"

"Sure, one on each floor."

Ally and Charlotte exchanged a look. As they left the kitchen Ally spoke in a murmur.

"The body could have been put into the chute on any floor. But my best guess is that it was done on the third floor."

"I find it hard to believe that this could be a crime of passion. It seems too well planned out, don't you think?" Charlotte pushed the button to call the elevator. "I think whoever did this knew exactly what they were doing."

"And had the access to pull it off." Ally stepped into the elevator after Charlotte.

"It doesn't exactly narrow down the list of suspects."

Ally watched the numbers change on the elevator. "No it doesn't. So, if we assume that the chute was the method used to move the body, then Dustin's body probably went through the door to the chute on his floor."

"Let's see if we can pin down this woman first, Brenna right?"

"Yes, Brenna Aberdene," Ally said as she looked at the details the chef had given her. "She should be in the room right across the hall from Dustin's." Charlotte stepped out of the elevator. Ally followed right after. Ally lingered for a moment beside Dustin's room. She got the feeling that even though it was locked, she could easily find her way in. However, her focus needed to be on the room across the hall. "Samples ready?" She looked over at her grandmother.

"Ready." Charlotte nodded. Ally knocked on the door with three firm strikes. After a few seconds the door swung open, and the very woman that Ally had locked eyes with when she had left Dustin's room, stood before her.

"Yes? What is it?"

"Hello. My name is Ally Sweet, and this is Charlotte Sweet. We'd like to share a few samples of chocolates with you, as we're trying to get the opinions of the guests staying at this hotel. Would you enjoy finding one of these chocolates on your pillow?"

Charlotte held out the samples.

"Oh." Brenna didn't take her eyes off Ally. "I thought you might be here for another reason."

"I am actually. I wanted to ask you a question as well." Ally held her gaze.

"What is it?" Brenna looked nervous.

"I'm here because you ordered two glasses of wine for your room on the night of the incident. I'd like to know if you drank them alone."

"I was in my room alone all night. I didn't mean to order two glasses of wine. They must have been sent up by accident."

"It's okay. You don't have to hide anything from us, Brenna. Maybe you met Dustin in the hallway. Maybe you thought it would be nice to have a drink with him?" Charlotte said.

"Nonsense. I didn't even see that man. All I know about him is that he ended up in the trunk of your car." She raised an eyebrow. "So, why are you questioning me?"

Ally cleared her throat. "Because I know that two glasses were found in his room. One with that exact same shade of lipstick on it," Ally said as she pointed to Brenna's lips.

Brenna narrowed her eyes. She gripped the door tightly and took a breath. "I don't know how the glasses got into his room. When I went downstairs I left them outside the door so they would be picked up. When I came back, the glasses were gone. I thought a staff member got them."

"I thought you stayed in your room alone all night?" Charlotte tilted her head to the side. "Now you're saying you left and came back?"

"Look, I told you and the police that I was alone for a reason. The man I was with, he's not exactly single. I don't want him to get pulled into all of this. It would ruin his life." She frowned and fixed her eyes to Charlotte. "Don't judge me. We're in love."

"Sure." Charlotte nodded. "So you had a glass of wine with your secret lover?"

Brenna rolled her eyes. "Yes. Then I went with

him down to the lobby to say goodbye. I was only gone about a half hour. When I came back the glasses were gone. I didn't think much about it, but if you say that there was a glass in his room with my lipstick on it, then someone must have taken them from the corridor and put them in there."

"Why would anyone do that?" Ally shook her head. "It doesn't make any sense."

"Maybe not, but I have never been inside that room, so either you're wrong about the lipstick, or someone took the glasses for a reason. Are you going to have to tell the police about this?"

"I don't know yet." Ally frowned. "I will do my best to keep it quiet, but if you had come forward in the first place it would have been a lot easier."

"Look, I'm sorry the man died, but I had nothing to do with that. An entire family will be devastated if this gets out."

"But you're in love, what do you care?" Charlotte lifted an eyebrow.

"I care. Just because we're in love, that doesn't change the fact that he has a family, he has responsibilities. It would break his heart to hurt them, and I don't want that to happen. I'm not asking you to understand, but consider the harm that will be done."

Charlotte nodded and looked over at Ally. "We will do our best to keep it quiet."

As they walked away from the door Brenna closed it behind them. Charlotte spoke in a low voice.

"What do you think? Did someone take the glasses?"

Ally stared at the laundry chute at the end of the hallway. "We already know that whoever did this had to have access to the car keys in the valet box, and know how the laundry chute worked. I don't think that a guest who has only been here for a few days would know that."

"Did you really find out that the lipstick was the same?"

"No, that was just a bluff. I wanted her to admit that she was drinking wine with someone. I just thought it would be Dustin, not some random, married man." Ally squinted at the laundry chute. "Plus, there's one other thing missing. Motive. If there was no history between them, why would Brenna kill him?" She shook her head. "No, as crazy as it sounds, the only thing that makes any sense to me is that someone put the wine glasses in Dustin's room on purpose."

"Someone made an effort to frame someone else, or at the least set a scene," Charlotte said.

"Not only that but if we assume that the wine glasses were taken from outside Brenna's room, then we have a likely timeline for the murder." Ally smiled. "That can give us a better idea of who was present at the time of the murder."

"What if she's lying?" Charlotte looked thoughtful. "We can't know for sure. The speech she gave about her lover is sweet, but it could all be a fantasy. Maybe she's trying to cover up for the fact that she was in Dustin's room."

"It's possible. Let's head back down to the lobby, I want to check on the staff that was working the bar. Perhaps one of them saw someone with Dustin."

"Maybe."

Chapter Ten

On the ride down with her grandmother in the elevator to the bar Ally was uneasy. It looked more and more like an employee at the hotel was responsible for the murder. She had to admit to herself that Denise was a very viable suspect.

"Mee-Maw, how well do you know Denise's mother?"

"Oh very." Charlotte nodded. "We haven't spent a lot of time together in the past few years, because she had retired and I hadn't. Life gets busy, you know? But we kept in touch here and there and now that we are both living at Freely Lakes I've started seeing her a lot more."

"Did anything ever happen in Denise's life that might make you think she could be capable of something like this?" Ally frowned.

"No, not at all, Ally. In fact, when your mother died, Denise offered to take you in. She cared about you that much, and was worried raising a young girl would be too much for me." Charlotte laughed at that. "She had no reason to be concerned about that, but it was a touching offer."

"I didn't know that." Ally was surprised. It occurred to her that her life would be very different if her grandmother had allowed that to happen. She couldn't imagine not having the guidance and love of her grandmother every day. Even though Charlotte was much older than the parents of most of her friends, Ally never noticed that. Charlotte's wisdom and sharp humor always kept their lives interesting.

"Oh, you had no choice my love." She patted Ally's cheek. "Ravenous lions couldn't have dragged you out of my arms. Though sometimes I did wonder if it was the right decision for you." She looked into Ally's eyes.

"It was." Ally smiled warmly at her. "It absolutely was." The elevator doors slid open and Ally waited for her grandmother to step out first. Her heart filled with affection as Charlotte stepped past her. They had their moments of disagreement, but when it came down to it, Ally couldn't imagine her life without her grandmother. The lobby was crowded with guests and staff as they scrambled to get back on track after the incident.

"While you are in the bar, I'll make the rounds with the guests. Maybe someone saw something," Charlotte said.

"Perfect."

Charlotte took one box of samples and Ally took the other. She veered off towards the bar while Charlotte wandered through the lobby.

If Ally thought the lobby was crowded, the bar was even more popular. Apparently a murder at the hotel was a good excuse to enjoy a drink. Ally noticed a harried looking bartender behind the bar. She walked over in an attempt to speak to her, but was pushed back by three men who wanted to get to the bar first. She raised an eyebrow and did her best to be patient. Once the rush died down a little she was able to get to the bar.

"Excuse me?"

The woman looked at her with a strained expression. "What can I get for you?"

"Actually, I have something for you." Ally held out the box of chocolates. "Would you like to try a few?"

"Oh yes! Thank you! I've barely had a chance to stop and eat. Ben, the manager, decided it would be a good idea to offer free drinks for everyone's trouble. I haven't been able to breathe between orders." She snatched up a few of the chocolates. "You're Ally right?"

"Yes. Did we meet before?"

"No, but I've heard about you."

"How?"

"Oh, the rumors are flying around here, trust me. Everyone has a theory about who took out Dustin."

"And you? Do you have a theory?"

"I don't have time to have a theory." The woman laughed. "I'm not even supposed to be working today."

"Were you working the night that Dustin was killed?"

"No, I wasn't. Another bartender was, which is why I'm here now."

"I'm sorry, I don't understand?"

"There was a new guy working, Phillip

Robinsons. I guess Ben didn't like what he was doing. Anyway, he was fired, and now I'm here covering his shift. I'm sure he'd rather be fired than dealing with this chaos." She sighed as a few people yelled for her at the other end of the bar. "I'm sorry I have to get back to it. Thanks for the candy."

"Take the rest of the box, I think you're going to need it."

"Thank you." She smiled.

Ally fought her way through another crowd of people that entered the bar. She stepped out into the lobby just as her grandmother walked towards the bar.

"Anything?" Charlotte looked at her with hope in her eyes.

"Nothing much," Ally said. "Just that the bartender that worked the night of the murder, no longer works here."

"I didn't get much, either. No one can recall seeing Dustin with anyone else."

Ally sighed and scanned the lobby again.

"Look, there's Ben." Ally grabbed Charlotte's

arm. "I'd love to find out what he thinks about this situation. I should go talk to him."

"He looks busy." Charlotte smiled slightly. "It's the perfect time to strike."

"You are so cunning, Mee-Maw."

"If he's distracted, he might tell you more than he normally would. I'll meet you in the parking lot when you're done. I want to look over the valet area again."

"Okay, I'll just be a minute." Ally walked towards Ben. He was occupied with three people that held out clipboards for his signature. She paused beside him as he took the last clipboard.

"Ben, I'm Ally Sweet from 'Charlotte's Chocolate Heaven'."

"Nice to meet you, Ally," Ben said but he did not sound genuine. "I am sorry but I can't talk about the chocolates right now."

"That's okay, I don't want to talk about that now. I was just wondering if I could have a minute of your time to ask you some questions about Dustin's death."

He scribbled his name on the piece of paper

and refused to look up at her.

"I don't have time for this. I've already spoken to the police."

"Oh, I understand that." Ally swallowed hard. She took a huge risk by confronting him. If he didn't like the way that she spoke to him he could kill the chocolate deal. "It's just that I've known Denise for a long time, and I'm certain that all of this must be some kind of mistake."

"I suppose you know more than the police?" Ben looked up at her and met her eyes. "Do you have some kind of information that they don't?"

"I just think that perhaps because Denise and Dustin had a brief relationship it's far too easy to simply assume that she was involved somehow. The judgment seems a bit rushed."

He shrugged. "That's what trials are for. In the meantime, I have to try to save the reputation of this hotel. Do you know what it's going to do to this place when it gets out that a staff member killed another staff member? It's bad enough that people want to believe a construction worker was killed before this place was even completely built.

I'm going to have all kinds of paranormal kooks trying to stay the night in Dustin's room."

Ally lifted an eyebrow. It seemed odd to her that Ben's biggest concern was ghosts. "Did you know Dustin well?" She held his gaze.

"Not well at all. Honestly, I don't know many of the staff members here well. The place is so new and my plate is full. At the moment it seems that the only people I really get to know are those that I have to fire."

"Like Phillip, the bartender?" Ally pursed her lips.

"Yes, like the bartender. Which means I'm under the gun right now to hire another one. Unless you have a suggestion for me, I need to get back to the hunt."

"Do you mind if I ask why you fired him?"

Ben licked his lips and then narrowed his eyes. "I'm trying to be patient here."

"It's the last question, I promise." Ally smiled.

"Fine. I fired him because he was stealing from me. He was lucky I didn't prosecute him. I gave him the opportunity to just walk out instead of ending up in handcuffs. So you see, I do try to be compassionate, but I can't tolerate a thief."

"Of course you can't. I understand you're busy. Thank you for taking the time to speak with me." Ally offered what she hoped was a professional smile. As she walked away she wondered if the impression she had left was a good one or if she had just blown the contract. By the time she met up with her grandmother in the parking lot, she was determined to track down the bartender and find out his side of the story about why he was fired. She thought about asking Kylie about it, but she didn't want Ben to see the two of them talking.

"How did it go with Ben?" Charlotte asked.

"I found out that he fired the bartender for stealing."

"Do you think he might be involved?"

"Denise said that Dustin wanted to meet with her about one of the employees. Maybe it was about Phillip. If he was stealing, maybe Dustin found out about it and wanted to tell Denise first. Phillip could have panicked and decided to kill him," Ally paused, "but the problem is he was fired before Dustin was killed. So why would he go to the trouble of killing Dustin if he'd already lost his job?"

"Maybe revenge?" Charlotte suggested. "People have killed for less."

"Maybe. But he took a big risk by coming back to the hotel to kill Dustin. Why would he do that? He could have waited for him outside, or even gone to his home."

"You're right, it's still possible though." Charlotte squinted at the cars lined up in the valet parking lot. "He probably wouldn't have had access to the keys to move your car."

"Unless he got them somehow or even worked together with the valet."

"No, I don't think so." Charlotte shook her head. "I think you're getting too far into a conspiracy. That would have been too hard to pull off and keep quiet with more than one person. I think our best theory is that someone on the staff did it, and they worked alone."

"But who? The only person I can think of that

has a motive is Denise." Ally cringed. "I hate to say it, but the more we dig, the worse she looks. I mean, her jacket was even wrapped around him."

"Yes, I know," Charlotte agreed. "That is why we need to be even more determined to get to the bottom of this. If we leave it to the Mainbry police they might just see it as an open and shut case."

"I'm just going to let Luke know what we found." Ally picked up the phone and dialed his number. It went straight to voicemail. She left a message saying that she wanted to update him on the case.

As Ally drove back to the cottage her mind churned through the new information they had gathered. It seemed to her that they had only added to the suspect list rather than narrowing it down. When she parked in front of the cottage she handed the keys back to her grandmother. Then snapped her fingers.

"Actually, can I have those back? I think I'm going to go have a talk with Phillip."

"If you're going to talk to the bartender, I'd rather you take Luke with you." Charlotte crossed her arms and held onto her van keys.

"Mee-Maw, I can't wait for him. He is busy with another case. Besides, he'll probably tell me to hand the information over to the Mainbry police department, and you know as well as I do where that will lead."

"Ally, listen to me." Charlotte spoke sternly. "You know that Luke will try and help you. He has a gun, you do not. He has a badge, you do not. What happens if you get to the bartender's house and he is drunk and violent? What happens if he thinks you're out to get him and decides to hurt you? How do you think Luke will feel knowing that he could have been there to protect you? The man cares about you, Ally, give him a chance to show that."

"I'm trying to." Ally sighed. "But I can't be dependent on him, Mee-Maw."

"This is the one part of the way I raised you that I regret." She frowned.

"My stubbornness?"

"No, my singleness." She hugged Ally close. "You never had the chance to see what a good healthy relationship is like. I wish you didn't think you had to be so strong all the time." She brushed her palm along Ally's cheek. "It really makes a difference to have a partner you can trust in this life, sweetheart. I know that you didn't have that with your first husband, but I promise that doesn't mean you can't have it with Luke."

"Mee-Maw! Now who's getting too far ahead of themselves? Luke and I are just friends, that is it. Nothing more."

"Is that really true, Ally? I mean, I can tell that he wants more. He's just waiting for the green light from you."

"I thought you didn't like cops?" Ally frowned and pulled away from her grandmother.

"It's true I get nervous around anyone who has the authority to put me in handcuffs, but Luke has proven to us that he's trustworthy, and that he is a good person beyond his badge, not to mention he's a great cop who might just have changed my view of things a little. I don't want to pressure you, Ally, but I don't want you to miss out on something great either. I just want you to think about it. All right?"

"All right." Ally smiled a little. She enjoyed the fact that her grandmother liked Luke so much. It made Ally like him even more. But there wasn't time to think about what that meant.

"It's late already why don't you have something to eat and try to sleep. I'm sure Luke will contact you by morning."

"But what happens if he hasn't?"

"We'll deal with it then," Charlotte said. "I'll pick you up in the morning and take you to the shop. Okay?"

"But if Luke can't come with me because of work I'm going to see Phillip by myself. Is that a good compromise?"

"It's a start." Charlotte laughed. "And by the way, your stubbornness is one of the many things I admire about you, Ally."

"Then you should know why I want to go talk to the bartender."

"And you should know that I am far more stubborn than you." Charlotte quirked her eyebrow.

"All right, all right. But I can't just sit around here waiting."

"I'll pick you up first thing to open the shop. Maybe the locals will know something."

"Good idea." Ally nodded. She stepped inside the cottage. Arnold and Peaches walked over to say hello. She patted them both and then fed them. Maybe the rumor mill would work in her favor.

Chapter Eleven

When Ally checked her phone the following morning, Luke still hadn't contacted her. She called him again, but it went straight to voicemail. She hung up before she left a message and then texted her grandmother saying she would walk to the shop. She wanted to clear her head.

After getting ready and feeding Peaches and Arnold she walked the short distance to the shop. When her phone chimed she looked at it quickly. It was from Luke.

Sorry I got caught up with something. I'll call you later.

Ally was relieved he was okay, but annoyed that he didn't seem to have time for her.

When she got to the shop her grandmother was already there.

"Morning, sweetheart," Charlotte said.

"Morning, Mee-Maw." Ally tried to sound

cheerful.

"Did you hear from Luke?" Charlotte asked.

"He just sent me a text to say he was caught up with something."

"Oh good. Hopefully he'll call you later and then you can see the bartender together."

"I hope so," Ally said as she began opening the shop.

After the morning rush Charlotte worked on making more chocolates to replenish their supply and Ally tidied up the display cabinets while trying to figure out who had the strongest motive. Denise topped the list because of the breakup. However, the bartender's desire for revenge might be on the list as well. If Dustin was the one to point out that he was stealing, then he probably had a score to settle. Ally straightened up the counter. She wiped down the surfaces and set about dusting the knickknacks on the shelf.

At that time of day, there were never very many customers. There was always a lull between lunch and school release. She actually enjoyed the quiet as it gave her a chance to think back over the events of the morning. If she was right about her hunch that the bartender knew something about the crime, she hoped that by the evening Denise would be out of jail. As she set down a wooden clock on one of the shelves the bell above the door rang. It signaled the entrance of three very familiar women. One by one, Mrs. White, Mrs. Cale and Mrs. Bing, walked into the shop. Ally smiled fondly at them as they headed straight for the sample platter on the counter.

"Afternoon ladies, you're early today."

"Oh, we couldn't wait any longer to get in here and try some chocolates," Mrs. Bing said.

"Here is a new flavor, caramel mousse," Ally said as she gestured to the samples. "You're the first customers to try them."

"Oh, how exciting." Mrs. White popped one into her mouth. Both of the other women did as well. Ally walked behind the counter and began to replenish the supply. Although the three women went through a lot of samples, they were not shy about purchasing large quantities for themselves and to give as gifts. It balanced out in the end, and the pleasure they got from being able to enjoy the samples was enough to make Ally smile.

"So, what do you think?" Ally asked.

"Mm." Mrs. Bing smiled around the chocolate? "So sweet, much better than that coffee disaster."

"It was not a disaster, it's my favorite," Mrs. Cale snapped. "But this is good, too."

"Very good." Mrs. Bing grabbed another sample just as Ally placed it on the platter. "Oh Ally, I'm just so anxious."

"Why?" Ally frowned. "Is something wrong?"

"Haven't you heard about the murder?" Her eyes widened and her voice fell into a dramatic hush.

"Of course she has, everyone has." Mrs. White clucked her tongue. "It is a terrible tragedy. A young man like that, gone too soon."

"It is." Ally nodded. "What have you heard?"

"Oh, just that an ex-lover was involved." Ally cringed at Mrs. Cale's description. "All those movies on television are right you know, love can be very dangerous."

"You think so?" Ally grinned at her. "I tend to agree."

"Pish, love is beautiful." Mrs. White sighed. "When it's with the right person of course."

Ally hadn't ever really thought about the three women being in love with anyone. They had always been a fixture in the shop and a big part of her childhood. But she barely remembered their husbands.

"Do you really think so, Mrs. White?" Ally leaned on the counter.

"I do. There's nothing more precious than the love of a genuine, honest man."

"If you get a good one." Mrs. Cale lifted her nose in the air. "Not all of us do you know."

"Enough of that chatter." Mrs. Bing waved her hand through the air. "I want to buy a box of these chocolates for Melly."

"Melly? Why?" Mrs. White raised an eyebrow.

"After what she is going through with her son, she deserves some of these chocolates."

"I don't know if that's a good idea." Mrs. White shook her head.

"Why not?" Mrs. Bing frowned. "It's not her fault her son got into so much trouble. The poor woman must be beyond embarrassed. The whole town will know about it soon enough. I tell you sometimes I think having children is a big joke on all of us."

"Careful there." Mrs. Cale tightened her lips. "Phillip insists that he is innocent."

"Why wouldn't he? It's not as if he's going to waltz around admitting to theft." Mrs. Bing shrugged. "Anyway, it doesn't really matter if he is or isn't. All that matters is that Melly has to face the embarrassment. Chocolate won't fix everything, but it might make things a little better."

"Who are you talking about?" Ally leaned forward and listened in to the conversation more closely. The three ladies were always gossiping about someone or something. They never meant any harm by it.

"We're talking about Melly Robinsons, and her boy Phillip."

"Phillip Robinsons?" Ally's eyes widened.

"Was he a bartender?"

"Yes, he was, until he was fired." Mrs. Bing shook her head. "Could you imagine? Stealing from your own place of work? Who does such a thing?"

"We don't know for sure that he did." Mrs. White crossed her arms. "Melly insists that he wouldn't have stolen from anyone."

"Melly insists because she's his mother." Mrs. Cale smiled. "All mothers want to defend their children, but they shouldn't always do that. If Phillip did wrong, then he needs to pay the consequences for it. Honestly, who would make that up?"

"Who knows." Mrs. White frowned. "You never can tell who someone's enemies are. Isn't that right, Ally?" She looked back at Ally.

Ally nodded, still stunned to discover that the man they discussed was the very same man she wanted to speak to.

"You just watch too many of those lawyer shows." Mrs. Bing rolled her eyes. "Innocent until proven guilty? Well, there won't be a trial for

Phillip. I can tell you this much, between Denise and Phillip, this town has a little too much scandal for my taste this week." She popped another chocolate into her mouth. "That's better." She sighed.

"Shush!" Mrs. White chastised Mrs. Bing. "Ally is friends with Denise you know."

All three women looked at her. "Yes, I am." Ally straightened up. "And I don't think that she had anything to do with this."

"If that's the case then it is a shame she is behind bars. But, if we can't trust the police to investigate these things, then what can we do?" Mrs. Bing clung to her purse, which Ally knew was filled with chocolates. "Someone has to be held responsible for that poor man's death."

"Sure, but it would be better if it was the right person. If you hear anything, you'll let me know, right?"

"Of course." Mrs. White patted the back of her hand. "I'll even check in on dear Rose, she must be so worried."

"Do you know her well?"

"Not really. We haven't talked much, but I'm sure she could use a friend."

"Will you take her some chocolates for me?" Ally handed her a package. "I don't want to upset her too much by going to visit. But I'd like to know that she has these."

"Absolutely." Mrs. White met her eyes. "You're such a sweet girl, Ally."

"Thank you." Ally replenished the chocolates on the sample stand. After a few more chocolates disappeared, the three women did as well.

Ally dialed Luke's number. She didn't want to wait any longer to talk to the bartender. His phone went straight to voicemail. Her lips tightened with frustration. Charlotte stepped out from the back.

"A friend of mine is in town, you remember Lola. She asked to meet me for dinner. Do you mind, Ally? She could drive me back to Freely Lakes after, that way you'll have the van."

"No, it's fine, Mee-Maw. Tell her I said hi and enjoy yourself." Ally smiled at her. Charlotte hugged her and then left the shop. Ally went through the motions of closing up the shop for the day. Her grandmother was right, she did get some valuable information and being around the chocolates had calmed her.

When Ally turned the lock on the door of the shop, it was only five o'clock. There was plenty of time to go visit the bartender and question him about his involvement with Dustin. But Luke still hadn't got back to her. She didn't want to miss the opportunity to speak with Phillip in case he decided to skip town.

When Ally got behind the wheel of the van she tried to call Luke one more time. His cheerful voice announced that he wasn't available to take her call. She hung up before she had the chance to leave an annoyed message. Luke has a job, she reminded herself. He's probably off saving lives, or taking down criminals. Maybe she could wait until the next morning. Luke was obviously still busy and probably working on an intense case.

As Ally neared the cottage she passed by one of the nicer restaurants in town. It didn't register until she was already past the car, that she recognized it. Luke was out to dinner again. He wasn't answering his phone, not because he had an intense case, but because he was busy with someone else. She tried not to let it get to her, but it did. Hadn't he told her to call him if she needed him? Obviously the case wasn't important to him. Obviously he didn't care that Denise rotted in a prison cell.

The more she thought about it, the more upset she became. She parked in front of the cottage and sat in the van for a few minutes. She wanted to go back and see who he was with, but she didn't want to embarrass herself and she was scared of what she might find out. It was easy to tell herself that she was only upset because the case was important to her. But she knew that wasn't the truth. If she was honest with herself she was upset because someone else had Luke's attention.

What didn't make sense to her was the way he behaved towards her. If he was with someone else why did he keep hinting at wanting more time with her? Was he just playing the field? Was she just the next woman on his list? Everything she knew about Luke told her that she was wrong about that. However, the fact that he still hadn't returned her call, and was not working, made it clear to her that he wasn't the person she thought he was. No matter what, she couldn't be distracted. She had to get Denise out. If Luke couldn't help her with that then she would have to do it herself. She pulled over to the side of the road and placed a call to Kylie. The phone buzzed only a few times before Kylie picked up.

"Hi Ally," Kylie said cautiously.

"Kylie, I was wondering if you could give me the address of Phillip Robinsons, the bartender that was fired?"

"Sure I can get you that. Is there a reason? Do you think he had something to do with what happened to Dustin?"

"I'm not sure yet. Having his address will help me figure it out."

"Okay, anything I can do to help. Yes, here it is. Do you have a pen?"

"One sec." Ally fished a pen out of her purse. "I'm ready." Ally jotted down the address that

Kylie read off to her. Once she had it written down she tucked the pen back into her purse. "Thanks."

"Are you going to his place?"

"I'm not sure yet. Kylie, has anyone reported an earring missing to the staff?"

"Oh, people lose jewelry all the time."

"Well, what about in the last few days? Has anyone lost just one earring?"

"What kind of earring?"

"A diamond stud."

"Where did you find it?" Kylie asked.

"Kylie, can you just let me know if anyone reported one missing please?"

"It might be easier for me to figure out if you told me where you found it."

"I'd rather not. Were any reported missing?" Ally frowned. Kylie's avoidance of the question made her more than a little suspicious.

"Not that I can see. I'll check again tomorrow morning."

"Thanks Kylie." She hung up the phone and stared at it for a moment. Why would Kylie be so hesitant about the earring? Was it possible that she knew more than she was letting on? Ally pushed the thought from her mind and focused on Phillip. Now that she knew she was on her own, there was no reason to wait for Luke. She drove to Phillip's address and found that it was a small duplex. She parked in the driveway and walked up to the door. After a quick glance around, she knocked. The curtain in the window beside the door fluttered, but no one opened the door. Ally waited a minute or two and then knocked again. When she was ignored, she knocked a third time, much louder. Finally, the door jerked open. A man in a sleeveless undershirt with ruffled hair leaned in the doorway. Ally recognized him right away as the man she had seen storm out on Ben at the hotel.

"Go away." He rubbed one of his eyes and groaned.

"I just need you to answer a few questions for me, please."

"Why should I?" He scowled at her. "Who are you?"

"My name is Ally. I'm a friend of Denise's."

"That chick that offed the security guy?"

"She did no such thing." Ally looked annoyed. "And his name was Dustin."

"Whatever. Why should I answer any of your questions?"

"Twenty?" Ally held out the bill. He sighed and snatched it out of her hand.

"What is it?"

"Did Dustin find out about you stealing from the hotel?" She squared her shoulders and studied his reaction.

"This again?" He shook his head. "I didn't steal from anyone. Not from the hotel, not from Ben, not from anyone."

"Did Dustin accuse you of it?"

"Dustin? Of course not. Dustin knew that I wasn't stealing. I'm the one that told him about what I saw."

"What do you mean, what you saw?"

He shoved the twenty dollar bill into his pocket. "All I knew was that there was money moving out of the hotel at night. When I would put together my deposit from the bar I took it to the manager's office. Ben had a drop box inside of his office for it. The café, the spa, the front desk, anyone who accepted any kind of payment would drop their envelopes in the drop box."

"That makes sense. How do you know money was missing?"

"I'm the last one to drop off the deposits. I'd been doing the deposits for about a week. Usually I have to wriggle the envelope a little bit to try to fit it into the drop box. Then I noticed that I didn't have to do that anymore. I was curious, so I peeked into the slot. There was nothing in there, just my deposit. I brought it up with Dustin, because he's the one in charge of security. He said he would look into it. Next thing I know Ben is in my face shouting about how he took a chance on me and I'd betrayed him." Phillip rolled his eyes. "Like I give a damn about loyalty. I needed money. I wouldn't risk my job by stealing. I wanted a paycheck." He grimaced. "I'm sure if I never said anything about the missing money I would still have a job."

"Or maybe Dustin found out it was you, and

he told Ben, and Ben fired you. Which made you want revenge." Ally folded her arms as she looked at him.

"Now you're trying to pin a murder on me?" Phillip laughed and shook his head. "I'm starting to think my mother was right. I need to get the heck out of this town. People here only care about rumors, not the truth. I gave Ben back his pin, and I left the hotel, like he told me to. I went back to get my paycheck and he even shortchanged me. I was annoyed, but I didn't really give him any trouble. So, if you think I stole something, or killed someone, then send the cops to get me. Until then, I'm going back to my nap." He shoved the door closed. She heard him engage the lock. Ally walked back to the van even more confused than when she had arrived. The theory of Phillip being involved in the murder was a good one, she knew that it was. But something about Phillip made her believe him.

As she got back into the van to drive back to the cottage, her phone buzzed with a text.

Ally, sorry I missed your calls. Can you stop by my place? I could use an update.

She smiled with relief at the text. If Luke was on a date would he really be texting her? She sent a text in return.

Five minutes away, be there soon.

Ally drove towards Luke's house as warmth built up within her. At least he remembered her. When she pulled into the driveway of his house she noticed his car parked there. As she walked towards the house she was surprised to hear Luke's voice through an open window.

"I think you should stay longer. Don't leave so soon."

Ally froze a few steps away from the door. Who was he talking to? His date? She moved a little closer to the window to listen in.

"Hold on, I'll get us a drink," Luke said.

Ally's stomach twisted. She paced back and forth to calm it. She couldn't hear who he was talking to. So he was in there with someone, someone who he didn't want to leave. Ally paced back and forth a few more times. She knew she shouldn't spy on Luke, and she certainly hadn't intended to.

Ally checked the text on her phone yet again. It did, as she thought, instruct her to meet him at his house. Why would he have her meet him there if he was going to be with someone else? Was he trying to confuse her? She thought about knocking on the door. He had invited her to come over, so it wasn't as if he wouldn't be expecting her. Still, she wasn't sure that she could keep her composure once he opened the door. After the encounter she had with Phillip she wanted to talk to him as soon as possible, but she also didn't want to witness Luke on a date with another woman.

Ally started to walk towards the door, then hesitated. If he was inside and alone with a woman, who knew what might be happening. They could be sharing wine, or even sharing his bed. She was sure that if she walked away she would die of curiosity. Maybe if she just took one little peek, she could put it all behind her. She paused in front of the door just before it swung open. Her heart skipped a beat. In front of her, through the mesh screen on the door, Luke looked different. He looked frazzled.

"I'm sorry, Ally, this isn't a good time," Luke said apologetically.

Ally's heart sunk. She had interrupted some kind of tryst, she was certain of it.

"I'm sorry, I got your text and I..."

"I know. I wanted you to come, I just didn't expect it to be like this. I'll explain later. All right? I just need you to go now."

Ally bit back annoyed words. She wasn't sure why he acted this way after all of the flirting he'd done. Was he just trying to bait her and then hurt her?

"Sure, I'll go." She spun on her heel and walked back towards the van. A part of her really expected that he was going to follow after her. However, when she reached the van and he was still inside the door, she knew that he wasn't coming. It hurt, she couldn't deny that. It hurt more than she expected it to. That was exactly why she kept herself at a distance. She forced herself not to dwell on it as she drove back to the cottage. She had enough on her mind. Not the least of which was getting her car back so that her grandmother could have her van back.

In many ways Ally felt as if her life had been hijacked the moment she opened the trunk of her car, and she needed to get it back. When she reached the cottage she was exhausted. She barely made her way into the living room before she collapsed on the couch. Peaches jumped up on the couch beside her.

"Just who I need to see." Ally sighed and stroked the cat's fur. "Peaches, life is confusing. I bet it's much more simple to be a cat."

Peaches looked into her eyes. She didn't blink. Ally smiled. "All right, maybe it's not so simple to be my cat." The cat nuzzled her hand.

Ally closed her eyes and willed her body to relax. The only way she could think through the case was with a calm body and mind. After a few deep breaths the pieces began to slide into place. By the time she fell asleep, she had a few theories running through her mind. It was enough to distract her from whatever Luke was up to.

Chapter Twelve

Early the next morning Ally headed to Freely Lakes. She didn't want to upset Rose and she had no intention to. She hoped Rose might have some insight about Dustin and Denise's relationship. It might give her the break she needed to piece together what had happened to Dustin. She checked the list at the front desk to find out which room Rose was in. Once she did she headed for it. She knew that her grandmother would have liked to tag along, but Ally wanted it to just be her and Rose. There might be some things Rose felt awkward talking about in front of Charlotte.

Ally knocked lightly on the door and waited for it to open. A moment later the door swung open. Rose leaned heavily on her cane as she eased herself down into a chair near the door. As she observed her, Ally noticed that her gray hair was uncombed. She leaned forward in her chair slowly which appeared to be painful. Unlike her grandmother, who was quite healthy, Ally could see that her senior years were taking a heavy toll on her body.

"Who are you?" She squinted towards the door.

"Ally Sweet."

"Oh Ally?" She smiled. "Come in, please. I can't believe I haven't had the chance to see you since you've moved back home. Look at you." She gasped and shook her head. "You look just like your mother."

"Thank you." Ally smiled. "Denise said the same thing."

"My poor girl." Rose held back her tears. "I feel so helpless. I can't get her out of jail. It's horrible that the police could just take her like that."

Ally sat down on a chair beside her. "I'm doing my best to help her, Mrs. Mitchell, I promise."

"Of course you are. You're such a good girl. Your mother would be proud."

"Thank you. Mrs. Mitchell, is there anything important you can tell me about Denise? Anything that she might have been upset about?

People that might have been upset with her?" She took Rose's hand with her own and stroked the back of it.

"I'm not sure. She didn't tell me too much about her troubles. I think she's always worried about me, and so she doesn't want to tell me things. I wish she would though."

"What about a man named Dustin?"

"Oh him?" Rose scowled. "He broke her heart."

"He did?" Ally raised an eyebrow. "I thought things ended well?"

"That's what she says, of course. Denise will never admit that anyone has hurt her. She's such a strong woman, nothing like me." She looked down at her wrinkled hands. "But she was going to marry that man. It's just that she wasn't quite ready and he wasn't willing to wait. That will break any woman's heart. Of course, I won't tell the police that. They will just try to use it to turn her into a killer."

"Mrs. Mitchell, it's important that you cooperate with the detectives."

"Absolutely not. When they let her out of jail, then I'll answer their questions. Denise was going to move back here to be with me. She wanted to create some distance between her and Dustin."

"Did she know if Dustin was seeing anyone else?"

"I don't know." Rose shook her head.

"What about any friends of hers? Did she mention anyone close?"

"Yes, Kylie of course. They are good friends. Kylie could probably tell you more about her than me. They were so close that Denise bought her a pair of diamond earrings for her birthday. I thought that was a little excessive, but Denise insisted that she wanted Kylie to have them."

"Diamond stud earrings?" Ally's eyes widened.

"Yes, I believe so. Very sparkly."

"Thank you so much for talking to me, Mrs. Mitchell."

"Of course. I do so enjoy seeing you, Ally."

"I will come back to visit soon, with Denise. Okay?"

"Wonderful." Rose managed a smile.

Ally rushed out of the room and away from Freely Lakes. Her heart pounded with anger as she drove to Mainbry. Nothing made someone look more guilty in her eyes than someone lying to her face. If that was Kylie's earring under the bed, then she had a lot to explain. When she burst into the lobby of the hotel she was relieved to see Kylie still at the front desk. She looked up at Ally as she strode towards her. Kylie's eyes widened the moment that Ally opened her mouth.

"I want to know why Dustin and Denise broke up." Ally stopped in front of the desk. She blocked Kylie in behind it.

"You think I know more about it than Denise told you?"

"I think that someone was in that room with Dustin. I think someone was in his bed and lost a diamond stud earring. A diamond stud earring that her friend gave her as a birthday gift." Ally met her eyes directly. "Maybe Denise didn't know anything about their meeting."

"Ally please." Kylie narrowed her eyes. "You

don't know what you're talking about."

"Then tell me."

"It wasn't until after they broke up. Okay?"

"You and Dustin?"

"It was just for fun. Just a way to blow off some steam."

"You were the one in the room with him?"

Kylie shook her head. "I didn't have any wine. That wasn't me. I don't believe that Dustin would have been with anyone else either. I have no idea where those wine glasses came from."

"Kylie, why didn't you tell the police this? Why didn't you tell me this?"

"Denise is a good friend of mine. Dustin and I weren't anything official. I just didn't want her to find out like that. I didn't want her to hate me." Kylie lowered her eyes. "It's not like I knew anything. When I left he was very much alive."

"Did he mention a meeting with Denise? Or an issue with one of the staff members?"

"No. We didn't exactly do much talking. Like I said, it was just a fling. When you said you found the earring, I was worried. Since I never told the police about being there, if they traced the earring back to me then they might suspect me."

"So, you've just been letting Denise sit in jail?"

"Ally, I didn't hurt Dustin. What good would it do for me to be in jail with her?"

"How do I know you didn't hurt him? Maybe it was more than just a fling to you. Maybe you overheard him making plans to meet with Denise, and you got jealous." Ally took a step back. Kylie had access to everything that she would need in order to pull off the murder. Now that Ally knew Kylie was in the room with him, there was no question that she was a suspect.

"That's not what happened." Kylie closed her eyes and covered her mouth for a moment. When she spoke again her voice was a whisper. "Dustin was heartbroken, all right? He wanted to marry Denise. He thought she was the one. He couldn't get over her. I was just a way to distract him, that's all. We both knew what it was. Denise is my friend, and if I thought at the time that she still had feelings for him I never would have been with Dustin."

"Then why don't you want her to know that you were with him? If she doesn't have feelings for him, why would she care?"

"You didn't see her face when she found out he was dead." She sucked in a sharp breath. "I think maybe she had more feelings for him than she let on. Denise wants her career lined up, she wants to be successful and settled before she considers getting married again. I guess that Dustin was just rushing things." She frowned. "Now that he's gone, I don't want her to know that on his last day alive he was with me. I just would hate for her to have that memory. Haven't you ever made a mistake, Ally?"

Ally nodded and swallowed hard. She wondered if she was making a mistake by not taking a chance on Luke. "Yes, I've made mistakes. But this may become a bigger issue than I can conceal, Kylie. Lucky for you I'm the one that found the earring not the police, but they will find it eventually and it's better to be upfront about your relationship before the police find out that the two of you were together. I think you need to consider telling Denise the truth."

"Maybe I will." She frowned. "But first she needs to get through this. If you really think me coming forward will make a difference in the investigation, then I will." She shivered. "I guess I am only looking out for myself."

"Don't do it just yet. I want to think about it a little. You're sure you didn't notice anything strange that day? Nothing about how Dustin acted? Words he had with anyone?"

Kylie stared off through the lobby for a moment. When she looked back at Ally her eyes widened a little.

"You asked me about Phillip right?"

"Yes. Why? Did Dustin have an argument with him?"

"No, not at all. In fact, he defended him. He saw Ben in the hallway when we were headed to his room. He noticed that Ben had a trainee pin in his hand. Dustin liked to be informed of any hirings or firings so he asked Ben about the pin. Ben said he had to let Phillip go because he was stealing."

"Wait a minute, Ben found out about the stealing, not Dustin?"

"Yes. At least that's what Ben said."

"Dustin had a different opinion?"

"He was pretty annoyed. He said that he vetted Phillip himself and was certain he wasn't stealing anything. Ben told him he had proof, he was the manager, and he had the final say."

"Did they argue about it?"

"No, not really. Dustin just walked away. Ben didn't seem to care that he had a different opinion." Kylie pursed her lips. "The two weren't exactly friendly with each other."

"Did Dustin say anything else at all to you about it that night?"

"Only that he didn't trust Ben. He thought he fired Phillip for a personal reason, and that it wasn't right to do that to someone. Then uh, we didn't talk much more after that." Her cheeks grew pink. "Please don't tell Denise. I don't want her to find out that we were together. I think she would forgive me, but our friendship would never be the same."

Ally's heart softened. She understood what it was like to want things to stay the same. "Kylie, I hope that you're telling me the whole truth now. Lying will not help Denise."

"I'm telling you the truth, Ally. If I thought it would have helped Denise, I would have told the truth much earlier. I just didn't know why anyone would need to know something like that."

Ally frowned as she walked away. Just when she thought she cracked the case wide open she really had no idea what the truth was.

When Ally returned home to the cottage she was exhausted. She curled up on her bed and closed her eyes. A few minutes later her phone rang. She saw that it was Luke, but she decided not to answer. She didn't want to think about who he was with in his house. She didn't want to hear the explanation or admit that she'd gone to talk to the bartender alone. She turned her phone to silent. As she began to drift off to sleep Peaches jumped up beside her. The soft purr of the cat eased her into a peaceful slumber.

Chapter Thirteen

Ally woke up the next morning with a sudden sense of urgency. Her chest was tight and her body covered with sweat. She wasn't sure why, until she recognized the feeling that she forgot something very important. She lay in her bed for some time as she processed through what she might have forgotten. Was there something she had overlooked in the investigation? Had someone's birthday slipped by while she was caught up in the murder? She grabbed her phone to check her calendar, it was sometimes the only way she was able to keep track of things. When she looked at the date, she saw that there was a reminder note.

Meeting with manager.

Her eyes widened. The reminder hadn't alerted her that morning because she had turned her phone on silent the night before. She had a meeting with Ben that morning at the shop. He wanted to tour it to be sure that the facilities were acceptable. Would he still be there? After the less than welcoming reception he offered her when she asked him some questions she wasn't sure. But he hadn't called to cancel, and she still wanted to land the account. Her grandmother was taking the morning off and if he showed up and Ally wasn't there then there would be no chance of him signing a contract. She hurried to dress and quickly fed Peaches and Arnold. Both of the animals looked up at her with wide, forlorn eyes. In all of the chaos she'd barely paid them any attention.

"I know, guys. I'm so sorry. I promise I will be home for lunch today and we can spend some time together. There's always something that needs to be done." She sighed and took a few minutes to pet each one. She added a few treats to their breakfast then grabbed an apple for herself. As she hurried out of the house she found herself uncertain of whether she was going to make it in time. She gunned the engine for the last few blocks. It would be embarrassing if she got pulled over, but she'd rather have a ticket than miss the meeting.

When she parked behind the shop there were no other cars present. A hint of disappointment caused her stomach to sink. Maybe he wouldn't come. Maybe she already blew the account with the questions she had asked about Dustin. She didn't regret it, but now she wondered if the timing couldn't have been better. As she opened up the store she prepared some chocolates just in case he did arrive. She put several out on the sample display. As Ally turned back towards the kitchen she heard the bell over the door ring. When she turned around, Ben stood just inside the door.

"I apologize for being late, I had some things to handle at the hotel."

"I understand." Ally smiled at him. "I appreciate you taking the time. I know things are difficult right now."

"That they are." He frowned. "But my guests still need chocolates on their pillows. Are you able to give me a tour?"

"Absolutely. This is the shop area. We serve coffee and tea for those that might want to stay and enjoy their chocolates. All of the artwork has been accumulated over the years, purchased from local artists and crafters."

"It's an amazing collection." He swept his gaze over the shelves and walls. "The shop has been open for some time then?"

"Yes, my grandmother opened it when she was a little younger than me, she still owns it, and now I am managing the day to day needs."

"How wonderful that it remains in the family. Maybe we could write up a little card about that. Tourists love that sort of thing."

"Good idea. That will be easy for me to do."

"Great." He tilted his head towards the kitchen. "Is that where you make the chocolates?"

"Yes. We also make a variety of baked goods and specialty treats." She led him towards the back. "There's this window that looks straight into the kitchen so that customers can watch us make the chocolates if they want to."

"Oh, my favorite!" He paused in front of the

counter and snatched a couple of the caramel mousse chocolates from the sample tray. "You don't mind do you?"

"No, please help yourself. That is a new recipe we're trying." The words caught in her throat. His comment echoed through her mind. How could they be his favorite if he had never tasted them before? She pushed the thought away and tried to focus on the tour. She walked him through the process and displayed the assortment of molds that he could choose from. "We can customize for any holiday or event that you might want us to."

"Sounds great." He nodded and slipped his hands into his pockets. "I don't see any reason not to go forward with this contract. I'll have the hotel's lawyer draw it up and hopefully we can get it signed by the end of the week. Does that sound good to you?"

"Yes, that sounds great." She grinned. "Thank you, Ben."

"Thank you. I'm glad that we were able to connect. I do wish it had been under better circumstances. For now you'll have to communicate through me until Denise's position is filled."

"Oh? Has she been fired?" Her stomach ached at the thought.

"She was arrested for the murder of a staff member. Ally, what do you think?" He arched an eyebrow.

"Well, she hasn't gone to court for it. I just thought maybe she'd have the opportunity to get her job back when she's proven innocent."

He chuckled and shook his head. "You may think that is a possibility, but I'm not so sure. Sometimes it's hard to know who to trust."

Ally studied him for a moment and then nodded. "Do you have any other questions about the chocolates?"

"I wonder if you can give me a list of the flavors I would have to choose from. I am certain that I will want to order these chocolates, in fact I would like to make a personal order as well." He popped the other caramel into his mouth.

"I can pack some up for you right now." She smiled but it was only for show. She found it very strange that the caramel chocolate was so familiar to him, since as far as she knew only Dustin had tried it at the hotel. Maybe Dustin gave him one of the chocolates? Her stomach churned as an awful thought struck her. Maybe Ben took them off Dustin's pillow after he murdered him. Her eyes widened and she looked away before Ben could notice. Heat rushed up through her cheeks as the terrible thought anchored in her mind. Was it possible that the man she was alone with was a murderer? Her hands trembled as she filled a box with caramel chocolates. When she tied the bow around the box her heart lurched. Was she appeasing a killer's sweet tooth? She turned around to find Ben right behind her.

"Excellent." His eyes locked to hers. "I can't wait to sink my teeth into these. I think we're going to have a wonderful relationship, Ally."

Ally's throat was dry as she nodded. "Thank you."

"I'll expect your first delivery by the end of the week."

He nodded to her, then turned and walked out

of the shop. Ally's heart raced. Should she stop him? Should she call the police? How could she do either when the only proof she had was the fact that he liked a chocolate that was on Dustin's pillow? Would anyone believe her? One person would, she knew. She dialed Luke's number. As soon as she heard the voicemail she winced.

"Luke, I really need to talk to you. I know you're busy, but I really need your help." She hung up the phone just as her grandmother walked through the door.

"Hi Ally," she called out.

"Mee-Maw, I..." Ally was interrupted by a delivery man walking into the shop.

"I'll take care of this, sweetheart. You can go and get some lunch."

"Thanks, Mee-Maw." Ally smiled. "I won't be long." Ally could fill her grandmother in on her suspicions about Ben after lunch, once she hopefully knew more.

Chapter Fourteen

As Ally left the shop she tried to work out what to do next. She wanted to get to Ben's office at the hotel. Maybe she would be able to find some kind of proof there, but she wanted to speak to Luke first. She tried to reach Luke again. Once more there was no answer. She grimaced and hung up the phone. She really wanted his opinion before she went ahead and discussed it with the Mainbry detective. The notion of Ben being the killer had never entered her mind before that and she found it hard to believe. If she could at least get Luke on her side then maybe the detective would listen to her.

Ally chewed on her bottom lip as she thought about being alone with him at the shop. If he was a killer, then he could have done anything to her. The important thing was that he didn't know she suspected him. As long as he didn't he hopefully wouldn't flee before he could be arrested. The stumbling block was the fact that there was very little proof. In fact there was no proof. Although he mentioned the chocolates being his favorite, and the only way he could have tasted them was off the pillow in Dustin's room, that wasn't going to hold up in court and wouldn't warrant an arrest.

Ally needed something more than that. She needed to know why Ben would want to kill Dustin. Was it a lover's triangle between Denise, Dustin, and Ben? If so why hadn't Denise mentioned it? If he had killed Dustin out of jealousy, why had he allowed Denise to take the fall for it?

When she reached the cottage she stepped inside and was greeted by a hungry pig and cat. As squeals and meows filled the kitchen she doled out some food for both. Her eyes caught sight of a few glasses in the dish drainer. The wine glasses. Unless Ben enjoys wearing lipstick after hours, he didn't share a drink with Dustin. Was someone in the room that made Ben jealous?

After she fed Peaches and Arnold she decided that she would do some research on the computer before she went to Ben's office. She settled in front of her computer. The best place to look to dig up some dirt was on social media. She looked up Denise's accounts and sifted through Denise's recent posts. There were several about her breakup with Dustin, all mild and complimentary. But there were none about the two of them getting back together. She also found not a single mention of Ben. Even though they worked together, they didn't appear to be friends and were not connected on any of the business accounts that Denise maintained. It seemed like a slim notion that Denise was involved with Ben.

Next, she turned her attention to Dustin's accounts. They were filled with condolence wishes to the family, and testimonies about what a good and honest person Dustin was. Ally became even more determined to solve his murder. It didn't appear to her that this was a man with many enemies. He also didn't have any connections with Ben on his account. What comments he posted about Denise were warm and considerate. There was no indication of a rift between the two.

In fact, as Kylie had mentioned, Ally suspected that they might have gotten back together in time.

Ally then searched for Ben. To her surprise there was not a trace of anything personal anywhere on the internet about him. She found him listed on the hotel's website as the manager. She also found a history of other hotels he had worked at. There were quite a few, but not any for more than a few months. That seemed very strange to her. Before she could look into it more Arnold nudged her knee so hard that Ally could no longer ignore him.

"All right, Arnold, why don't you play outside for a bit and I'll take you for a walk later." She jumped up and hooked a thumb in his collar. With fast steps she pulled him towards the back door. Peaches jumped up in the window beside the door and gave a deep purr.

"What is it with the two of you?" Ally shook her head. "One minute you love each other the next you can't stand each other."

Ally opened the door so that Arnold could go outside. Just as she was about to close it, Peaches jumped down and bolted out through the door.

"Peaches! Get back here." She sighed and started after the cat. Peaches ran right under the shed. Ally couldn't reach her there. All there was to do was wait. Ally frowned. She knew that if she tried to catch Peaches she would just run away. It was better to leave her then she would hopefully just come back inside on her own.

Just as Ally was about to walk inside she noticed the mailman drop off a letter in her mailbox. She waved hello and walked over to the mailbox and got the envelope out. As she held it in her hand she remembered Phillip mentioning the envelopes full of money that he deposited in Ben's office. He said he had spoken to Dustin about it. Her eyes widened. Could Ben have been stealing? Did Dustin confront him about it? But that didn't add up with what Kylie had said.

Ally walked inside and left the door open in case Arnold and Peaches wanted to come back inside. Ally wanted to investigate more about Ben. As she sat back down at the computer her cell phone began to ring.

"Hi Luke. I've been trying to reach you."

"I know, I'm sorry. I had to have my phone off for a meeting. Is everything okay?"

"I'm not sure. I think I might have figured out who is responsible for Dustin's death."

"Who do you think it is?"

"Ben."

"The manager?"

"Yes."

"Why do you think that?"

"Just hear me out, this will sound odd at first." She filled him in on her suspicions. By the time she finished, the silence on the other end of the line left her unsettled. "What do you think, Luke?"

"I think that we have to find some actual proof to tie him to Dustin's murder. If we can't do that then there's no chance of getting an arrest warrant."

"What about fingerprints or DNA?"

"He's the manager of the hotel, not only does he have the right to be in any room of the hotel, he was with the police officers all through the crime scene. Unless we find his DNA under Dustin's fingernails, which we won't because there wasn't any, we can't prove that he caused Dustin any harm. Ally leaned back in her chair and groaned.

"I've been all through his history. There are no obvious red flags. The only thing I found is that he has worked at quite a few hotels in the past and he doesn't seem to work at them for very long."

"Interesting."

"It is. But I don't know if that means anything. I'm going to look harder and try and see if there's anything else I can come up with."

"I'll ask one of the techs at the station to follow up on it. It might be a good lead. In the meantime, stay out of his way. No need to draw his attention to you."

"That might be kind of hard. I'm supposed to meet with him and his lawyer later this week to sign a contract."

"You're going through with that?"

"What if I'm wrong? I can't risk losing such a good deal for the shop. Besides, the contract isn't with him, it's with the hotel." She sighed. "I know it probably isn't right for me to think about things like that with all that's going on, but I can't ignore my responsibility to the shop."

"No, I suppose you can't. Hopefully we'll have all of this figured out before that meeting. What are you doing for the rest of the day?"

"I'm going to head back to the shop in about a half hour. I just came home to feed the animals."

"Maybe I'll drop by later?"

"Sure." She paused and fiddled with her phone. "I'd like that. If you're available."

"All right, I'll text you when I'm on my way."

"Great. Thanks Luke. Let me know if the tech finds anything."

"Of course I will."

Ally headed back outside. She felt a little calmer since she had actually spoken to Luke. After a short chase she caught Arnold. She rubbed his head and ears. As she stood up she gazed down at the pig. He stared at her for a moment then he began to snort and squeal. "Arnold, what is it?" Ally raised an eyebrow. Just as she started to turn to look over her shoulder a hand wrapped around her from behind. It smoothed tape across her mouth before she had the chance to scream. She struggled against the arms that tightened around her and pinned her arms at her sides. She tried to kick her feet back against the legs that she knew were there, but she missed.

Ally was pulled back across the yard towards the cottage. She shrieked against the tape. Even though it muffled the volume of her screams she hoped that someone might hear her. She didn't want to be taken into the house where there was less chance that she would be found, she wanted to be out in the open.

Rather than going through the backdoor, she heard the creak of the doors to the crawl space. Her stomach sank. No one would think to look for her there. She struggled even harder. A fist struck her hard in the stomach. She buckled in response to the sudden pain. He took advantage of the moment and shoved her down through the doors of the crawl space. Ally scrambled to her feet, but it was too late. He barreled down after her and shoved her back down in the dirt. Ally felt her phone fall out of her pocket.

"Don't you make a sound." He grabbed her by the ankles and jerked hard. Ally struggled to see through the darkness and the tears that filled her eyes. Just as she had suspected, it was Ben that wrapped a rope around her feet and tied it so tight that her feet began to go numb.

"Don't please, stop!" Whether he heard her through the tape or not, she didn't know. He grabbed her hands and jerked them hard behind her back. As the second rope wrapped around her wrists, Ally's tears fell harder. She could barely breathe from the panic that flooded her and her taped mouth made it even more difficult. As he waited for any opportunity to harm her, it dawned on her that Ben was going to have to kill her. She saw his face, she knew he was the one to put her in the crawl space. He would never risk her speaking to the police. She squirmed and tried to roll away from him. He placed his foot in the square of her back.

"You got into business that was none of your concern. Now I have no choice but to get rid of you. I'm sorry, it was my mistake. I never should have mentioned the chocolate. I was so careful to make it look as if Denise killed Dustin. But I was reckless, all because of those candies. You see, I brought my box with me to the local diner when I went to have some lunch. When I opened it up to have one, one of the ladies there mentioned that those were a brand new flavor, that no one else besides her and her two friends had tried those chocolates. Then I remembered that Lisa mentioned that only Dustin's room had those chocolates. You're a smart woman, Ally. I knew it wouldn't take long for you to put two and two together. Unfortunately, I made a mistake, and now you have to pay for it." His cell phone rang. "What now?" He sighed. He tightened the ropes on her despite her struggle. Then he was gone. Her heart pounded. Was he going to take the call and come back? Was he going to leave her there?

As soon as the doors closed behind her darkness flooded the crawl space. She tried to get free of the ropes around her hands and feet, but they were tied tight. She heard her phone vibrate as someone called her. She struggled to reach it but she couldn't with the ropes around her hands. As loud as she could she screamed against the tape over her mouth. However, the sound that was emitted would never be heard outside the crawl space. Sure, she would be missed soon. Either her grandmother or Luke would notice that she hadn't been around. But that didn't mean that she would be found.

Chapter Fifteen

As Ally lay in the crawl space all she could hear was her own heartbeat. She closed her eyes and wondered how she would escape. If she could escape.

In time Ally knew that the crawl space would be searched. But by then it would probably be too late. She had no idea when Ben might come back for her, or what he planned to do when he did. Was he just going to leave her there? Would he try to burn down the whole cottage? Her stomach ached at the thought. She had many good memories connected to the cottage, and it had never occurred to her that she might not have the chance to make any more. A few minutes later she heard footsteps above her head. Her breath caught in her throat as she heard her grandmother's voice. She wanted to scream.

"Have you tried tracing her cell phone?"

"I can't just do that. But I am trying to get in touch with someone who can. She hasn't been in touch with anyone she knows?" The sound of

Luke's voice was muffled by the floor, but Ally was relieved to hear it. She screamed as loud as she could against the duct tape, but only succeeded in tearing the skin of her lips.

"No one has heard from her. This is very unlike her. She was meant to come back to the shop. Not only that, but the animals were out in the yard when I got here. She would never leave them out if she wasn't here. I promise you, Luke, she did not leave this house of her own free will. Someone took her."

"But who?"

"I don't know. She suspected the bartender, Phillip."

"He's been cleared. His alibi held up. He was with a group of friends at a bar blowing off steam after being fired. I don't see how he could have been in two places at once. So, I think he's in the clear."

"Maybe you should go talk to him just in case."

"I will. But she called me this afternoon and mentioned that she suspected the manager, Ben, so I'll try to talk to him, too."

"Really?"

"Something about some caramel chocolates."

"Oh no, Luke, what if we can't find her?"

"I will find her."

"You don't know that."

"I do!" His voice grew stronger. "I promise you, Charlotte, I'll find her and bring her home."

"Please do, Luke, please do."

"I'm going down to the station to get that trace done on her cell phone. You stay here in case she comes back."

"Okay, I will." Ally's heart sunk. She continued screaming, but it didn't work. She couldn't make a sound that was nearly loud enough. She willed Luke to think about looking in the crawl space. He had no reason to, but she hoped that he would.

"I'll be back."

"Okay. Oops, watch the cat she's trying to get out."

"Watch it, Peaches!" Luke's voice raised. "Oh no, she's out!"

"And Arnold's right behind her!" Charlotte groaned. "This is not the time for this! Get back here right now, Arnold!"

Ally heard the squeals. She heard Charlotte as she fussed at Peaches.

"You bad, kitty, you shouldn't have shoved open the door like that. Now get back inside. You too, Arnold. I'm sorry, Luke, they must be worried about Ally, too."

She could hear Arnold's feet running back and forth across the doors of the crawl space.

"It's okay, let me get Arnold for you."

Ally's eyes widened. This was it, this was her last chance to get Luke's attention. She rolled over in the crawl space and wiggled in the dirt. When her feet connected with a pipe, she was flooded with excitement. As hard as she could she kicked the pipe. Her shoes were too soft to make a loud thump, but she hoped that it would be loud enough for Luke to hear. Again and again she kicked the pipe. Arnold snorted as he continued to run. Ally's heart pounded and she kicked harder. Please Luke, please look for me, she screamed within her mind. Just when she thought her legs couldn't lift again she heard his voice right outside the crawl space.

"What is that?" Luke asked.

She heard the metal doors part and wondered if it might be a dream. Then there he was, Luke, his eyes filled with concern peered down inside the crawl space. When he saw Ally his eyes widened.

"She's here, Charlotte! She's here! Call an ambulance!" He climbed down into the crawl space and pulled a knife from his pocket. Carefully he cut through the ropes. She reached up and tugged at the tape on her mouth. It didn't matter that her skin burned from the tear, she pulled it off as fast as she could. Luke wrapped his arms around her.

"Are you okay? Are you hurt?"

"I think I'm okay." She clung to him. "Thank you for coming, Luke, thank you for finding me. I didn't think anyone would." His arms tightened around her.

"I'm here, Ally. I would never have stopped

looking. But it was Arnold who knew right where you were." He shook his head in amazement. "That is one good watch pig and watch cat you have there. Peaches even pushed the front door open for Arnold to get out." He brushed her hair back from her eyes. "Tell me what happened. Who did this to you?"

"It was Ben, the manager from the hotel. He's the one that killed Dustin."

"You're safe now." He held her close for another long moment. Charlotte rushed out of the house towards the crawl space just as they climbed out.

"Ally? Are you okay?"

"I'm okay." Ally managed a smile, but still held onto Luke.

"Ally, I can't believe that you were here the whole time. I'm so sorry. I should have known. You poor thing, you must have been terrified."

"I'm okay, Mee-Maw. There was no way that you could have known. I'll be fine. I just want to make sure that Ben is behind bars and Denise is free."

"I'm working on that now." Luke held his phone to his ear. Ally could tell by the tension in his gaze that he was not getting the answers that he wanted.

"They don't know where he is, do they?" Ally's chin trembled. "He's gotten away, hasn't he?"

"We don't know that for sure, Ally. He could just be in hiding," Luke said. "He probably didn't think anyone would find you."

"But I'm so glad that we did." Charlotte squeezed her hand and looked into her eyes. "I should have known."

"Mee-Maw, you know you couldn't have."

"Maybe." She sighed. "But Arnold and Peaches knew."

Ally stared off down the street for a long moment. When she looked back at Luke he hung up the phone.

"I know that look. What is it?" Luke asked.

"Maybe he doesn't know that you found me," Ally said.

"He probably doesn't." Luke shrugged.

"Then I should go back down into the crawl

space, and you two should act like you never found me."

"What?" Charlotte shook her head. "No, I don't think that's a good idea at all."

"It's the only way that we're going to catch him. We have to draw him out."

"Ally, we're not going to use you as bait." Luke crossed his arms. "That is out of the question."

Ally raised an eyebrow and shook her head. "That decision is not only yours to make, Luke."

"It is." He narrowed his eyes. "I'll have you in handcuffs before I let you go back down there."

Ally clenched her teeth. She knew that Luke meant well, but she was not one to be told what to do.

"Luke, you're not thinking clearly. If you were, you would know that this is the best thing we can do. The only option that we have. Otherwise Dustin's killer gets away with everything."

Luke stared at her. His eye twitched. Though his expression remained hard, his demeanor softened.

"It's still a bad idea."

"I'll be fine. You'll be right here with me. I won't be alone. He won't have the chance to hurt me."

"You can't seriously be thinking about this." Charlotte stepped between them. "The very thought of you being trapped back under the house." She gulped and shook her head. "I can't even consider it."

"Mee-Maw, I will be safe. If I don't do this, then we'll never know when he might come back. He will have the upper hand and we will have to live in fear. Is that what you want?"

"No, it's not." Charlotte sighed. "If Luke thinks that we can keep you safe, then I guess we should do it. But Ally, won't you be scared?"

"Maybe." Ally bit into her bottom lip. The real answer was, absolutely. The thought of being in that dark crawl space again made her stomach twist with fear. But it was what had to be done. She wasn't going to be afraid of Ben for the rest of her life. If he wasn't in jail she would always be looking over her shoulder.

"I need to go back in before he spots me out here. Both of you will have to stay out of sight. Luke, you'll need to let the Mainbry detectives know not to interfere."

"I will." His eyes widened as if the realization of what they were about to do dawned on him. "But there is no way you are going back in there."

"I have to," Ally said. "Otherwise we will never catch him."

"No, what we will do is we will hide in the house so you are out of sight," Luke said. "When he opens the door to the crawl space I will come and get him."

"That's a much better idea." Charlotte nodded.

"Okay," Ally agreed.

"I'm going to watch for him like a hawk, Ally," Charlotte said. "He won't get near you."

"Thanks Mee-Maw." Ally smiled at her. "It's all going to be just fine."

"It better be." Charlotte pursed her lips.

"We need to make sure that Arnold and Peaches stay inside so they don't get in the middle of anything," Luke said.

"Okay." Charlotte nodded.

"I will let the responding officers know what we're doing, then they will help keep an eye on what is happening." Luke pulled out his phone and made the call. When he had finished he turned to them. "Okay, let's go inside." Luke gestured towards the house.

"What if it doesn't work? What happens if he figures out that I'm out?" Ally asked.

"He won't, but we need to get inside before he does," Luke said. "We should go now though, he could be coming back any minute."

"I just need to get my phone, it's still in there," Ally said as she turned towards the crawl space. As she looked into it she got scared.

"I'll get your phone," Luke said.

"I'll meet you in the cottage," Charlotte said as she walked inside.

As Luke stepped in Ally felt a hard shove from behind. She was pushed into the small space behind Luke. She fell on top of him.

Luke went to loosen his holster.

"Don't, or I'll shoot her," Ben said as Ally turned around to face him.

Luke grasped her hand to reassure her as they were huddled together.

Ben gazed down at them. "Well, look at this, isn't that lucky." He laughed. "A two for one. Perfect. I was a little worried about what she might have told you." He moved the gun and pointed it straight at Luke. "Don't you move a muscle, Ally! It's Luke's turn first." Ben held the gun on Luke.

Ally froze at the sight of the gun pointed at Luke. She was sure the other officers had to be in place, but no one was coming to help.

"Don't hurt him, Ben. You don't have to do this."

"Actually, yes I do. Just like Dustin had to go. He got into my past and saw that I wasn't who I claimed to be. I have embezzled from several other small hotels. He was going to interfere in my life, and I couldn't let that happen. I can't let you get away with it either. I mean this should never have come back to me. I even put the wine glasses in the room so it would look like a lover's argument."

"Why did you put the body in my car?" Ally asked. She was curious, but she also wanted to keep him talking. If he was talking he wasn't shooting.

"That was just unfortunate for you. I wanted to drive the body out in my car, no body no evidence, but the valet came downstairs and I was scared he was going to catch me. Your car was the closest so I grabbed the keys and put it in. I was going to move the body to mine before you left. But you left so early I didn't have a chance."

He started to pull back on the trigger. Ally threw herself on top of Luke as a thud filled the air. She was sure that she or Luke had been shot.

"Ally?" Charlotte's voice drifted down to her. Luke moved under her body.

"Ally, I'm okay." He eased her off him. "Are you okay?"

"I think so."

She looked up at Ben's body, which was sprawled out in the grass at Charlotte's feet. In one hand she held a large frying pan, in the other she had her cell phone.

"The coast is clear, but you're going to need an ambulance for this scum."

"Mee-Maw?" Ally managed to get to her feet. "What did you do?"

"The police were too far, they're lined up on the street. I was closer. When I saw him push you in there with his gun on you I knew I couldn't wait. So I grabbed Bertha, and took care of the problem."

"Bertha?" Luke narrowed his eyes as he climbed out of the crawl space. He offered Ally a hand to help her out of the space.

"The frying pan." Ally smiled. "Its name is Bertha."

"Of course it is." He laughed.

Chapter Sixteen

The backyard was flooded with police officers. Ally remained close to Luke as Ben was treated and escorted to an ambulance.

"Well, Mee-Maw, I guess Bertha can still do some serious damage."

"Yes, and make the best pancakes. Anyone hungry?"

Ally laughed. "I'm sure that Luke has things he has to do."

"No, actually." He looked over at her. "There's nowhere I'd rather be. I'm starving." Ally hooked her arm through his.

"Then please join us. Mee-Maw doesn't know how to make just a few pancakes."

"It isn't right." Charlotte shook her head. "Besides, I'm sure a few of these officers are hungry, too."

"Maybe." Ally grinned. She led Luke into the house. While Charlotte prepared the batter, Luke leaned across the table and spoke in a whisper.

"So, about that date."

"Breakfast?" She smiled. "We're having pancakes right now."

He sighed and slouched back in his chair. She smiled as sweetly as she could. He shook his head and smiled back at her.

"It'll do. For now."

"For now." Ally reached across the table and took his hand. "Thanks for everything, Luke."

He smiled in return and started to lean towards her, but before he could get too close his cell phone began to ring. Ally pulled her hand back as he reached for his phone. She recalled the dates he'd been on recently and knew the moment that he turned his head to answer the phone that it must be her.

"Excuse me, just a minute." He stood up from the table and walked away with the phone pressed hard against his ear. Ally tried to ignore the tears that bit at her eyes. Was she crazy for feeling so hurt that he took her call right in front of her straight after he had rescued her? She was the one that pushed him away. She tried to remind herself of this, but her emotions took over. He glanced back at her once, and then walked towards the door. He looked out through it at the officers that were still investigating the crawl space and other areas of the property. To her surprise the muscles along his shoulders rippled. Something had him tense.

"This isn't the best time. Will you just listen to me?" He paused and his muscles tightened more. "I'd rather you didn't. Does that matter?" He shook his head. "Fine. Just give me a minute." He hung up the phone, then turned back to face her. Ally braced herself for whatever might come next. He met her eyes with a grim expression. "I didn't want this to happen this way exactly, but I don't have much of a choice now, Ally. There's someone here that I would like you to meet."

Ally's eyes widened. Was he really going to introduce his girlfriend to her? Her stomach twisted. Could she be civil, or was she going to end up embarrassing herself in front of him?

"Oh sure, it's fine, I mean, I understand, Luke." She cleared her throat. "I want to meet anyone who is important to you."

He narrowed his eyes. "It's complicated."

Her heart sunk. Only romance was ever complicated. She nodded without saying another word. There was a light knock on the door. Luke turned to it, just as Charlotte stepped back into the room. She must have sensed Ally's discomfort as she came and stood close to her. Luke sighed and opened the door. Ally expected a beautiful woman to step through the door into the kitchen, someone exotic and perfect, someone much more deserving of Luke's attention. To her surprise that was not who walked through the door. In fact it wasn't a woman at all, but a man. He reached up and pulled off a dirty baseball cap. The moment his hazel eyes met hers there was no question in Ally's mind that this man was related to Luke.

"You must be, Ally." His lips spread into a wide, slightly amused smile. "I've heard so much about you."

"Trey." Luke's voice filled with warning as he stepped up right beside the man. Ally guessed that he was a few years younger than Luke.

"I didn't say anything." He shot an innocent

smile in Luke's direction. Ally looked between the two as confusion built within her. Charlotte gave her shoulder a squeeze.

"I'm Charlotte." She looked at Luke. "And this is?"

Luke grimaced. "Charlotte, Ally, this is my brother, Trey."

"Brother?" Ally raised an eyebrow. She didn't think Luke had ever mentioned a brother, but then again he never really mentioned much about his past or his family.

"He doesn't talk about me much, does he?" Trey winked at her. "He's not the bragging type, right?" He clapped Luke on the back.

"Stop." Luke shot him a look.

"Relax Luke. I heard all of the sirens. I just wanted to make sure that you were okay. Plus, I wanted to finally meet the famous Ally." He smiled at her again. Ally looked from Trey to Luke. His cheeks were hot with embarrassment. She stood up from the table and offered Trey her hand.

"It's a pleasure to meet you, Trey."

"Thanks." He took her hand, but instead of shaking it, he drew her hand to his lips. He kissed the back of it. Ally cleared her throat. Luke rolled his eyes. "See, I didn't bite, did I, Ally? I've been trying to get Luke to introduce me to you all week, but he's been hiding me away."

Ally frowned as she glanced over at Luke. She had to wonder why he didn't want her to meet his brother.

"I'm glad to have the chance. Your brother is a lifesaver. Literally."

"He's hard to live up to." Trey grinned and looked back at Luke. "Golden boy that he is."

"That's enough, Trey. Ally's had a traumatic day, she needs to rest." Luke put a hand on his brother's shoulder.

"You're right." Trey nodded and met Ally's eyes. "You're pretty brave. That's good. You're going to need to be with this guy." He gave Luke a playful punch to the midsection.

"It's okay, Luke," Ally said. "I bet Trey would like some pancakes. What do you say, Trey? There are plenty to go around."

"I say, it's a date." He grinned and winked at Luke. "Told you I could get one with her first."

"Keep quiet, Trey!" Luke demanded.

Ally put a hand over her mouth to hide her laughter. Charlotte returned to the stove as Trey pulled out a chair and sat down across from Ally.

"How long are you in town for, Trey?" Charlotte asked.

"Not long." Luke sat down beside him.

"He's right. I've been traveling so I just came for a quick visit before I go back home." He glanced over at his brother. "Although, it's been nice spending some time with my brother again."

Luke took a deep breath and leaned back in his chair. For the first time since Trey walked through the door Ally saw him smile.

"Yes, it has been. I hope that it won't be so long between visits," Luke said.

"It won't be." Trey held his gaze.

"And you make sure you keep in touch this time," Luke added.

"I said I would and I will." Trey looked at him earnestly.

Luke nodded and accepted a plate of pancakes from Charlotte. "Thank you."

"Anything for our hero." Charlotte smiled at him.

"Please don't." Luke looked away and his cheeks reddened again.

Trey glanced at Charlotte as she put his pancakes down in front of him. "Thank you."

As Ally watched the two brothers dig into their pancakes, she was more intrigued than ever. Luke had an entire life that she knew very little about. Maybe it was time she stopped avoiding her feelings so much, and got to know him better. He met her eyes across the table. She smiled at him. No matter the chaos that happened around her, when he smiled back, everything was right with the world. Soon Denise would be released, the murderer would be in jail, and hopefully the chocolate shop would still have an account with the hotel.

"Mee-Maw, I think we're going to have to make some more chocolate cupcakes. Rose and Denise are going to need to celebrate."

"You're absolutely right." Charlotte smiled as she set a plate of pancakes in front of Ally. "We'll be sure to double the batch."

The End

Chocolate Cupcake Recipe

Ingredients:

2 ounces semisweet chocolate

1 cup all-purpose flour

1 1/2 teaspoons baking powder

1/3 cup unsweetened cocoa powder

5 ounces butter at room temperature

1 cup fine sugar

2 large eggs at room temperature

1 teaspoon vanilla extract

1/2 cup milk

Whipped Ganache Frosting:

12 ounces semisweet chocolate

1 cup heavy cream

Preparation:

Preheat oven to 325 degrees Fahrenheit.

Line a muffin tin with paper cupcake liners. This recipe makes 24 cupcakes.

Gently melt chocolate over a low heat preferably in a double boiler. Once it is melted set it aside to cool.

Sift the flour, baking powder and cocoa powder into a bowl and stir to combine.

Cream butter and sugar until light and fluffy.

Beat the eggs into the butter mixture one at a time until well incorporated. Beat in the vanilla extract.

Fold in some of the dry ingredients alternating with some of the milk. Keep folding in until all combined. Do not overmix.

Fold in the melted chocolate.

Spoon into paper liners. Only fill each liner until about 2/3 full.

Bake for 14 - 18 minutes or until a skewer inserted into the middle comes out clean.

Leave to cool in the pan for 20 minutes then transfer to a wire rack to cool completely.

To prepare the whipped chocolate ganache frosting chop up chocolate and place in a heatproof bowl.

Heat cream on the stove until it is just beginning to simmer.

Pour the cream over the chocolate and then leave for about 2 minutes so the chocolate can begin to melt. Stir the mixture slowly until the chocolate has completely melted and is mixed with the cream.

Let the ganache cool in the fridge for an hour or until it can hold its shape. Whisk the frosting for 3-4 minutes.

Spread a spoonful or pipe onto the top of the cupcakes.

Enjoy!

More Cozy Mysteries by Cindy Bell

Chocolate Centered Cozy Mysteries

The Sweet Smell of Murder

Sage Gardens Cozy Mysteries

Birthdays Can Be Deadly

Money Can Be Deadly

Trust Can Be Deadly

Ties Can Be Deadly

Rocks Can Be Deadly

Dune House Cozy Mysteries

Seaside Secrets

Boats and Bad Guys

Treasured History

Hidden Hideaways

Dodgy Dealings

Suspects and Surprises

Wendy the Wedding Planner Cozy Mysteries

Matrimony, Money and Murder

Chefs, Ceremonies and Crimes

Knives and Nuptials

Mice, Marriage and Murder

Heavenly Highland Inn Cozy Mysteries

Murdering the Roses

Dead in the Daisies

Killing the Carnations

Drowning the Daffodils

Suffocating the Sunflowers

Books, Bullets and Blooms

A Deadly serious Gardening Contest

A Bridal Bouquet and a Body

Bekki the Beautician Cozy Mysteries

Hairspray and Homicide

A Dyed Blonde and a Dead Body

Mascara and Murder

Pageant and Poison

Conditioner and a Corpse

Mistletoe, Makeup and Murder

Hairpin, Hair Dryer and Homicide

Blush, a Bride and a Body

Shampoo and a Stiff

Cosmetics, a Cruise and a Killer

Lipstick, a Long Iron and Lifeless

Camping, Concealer and Criminals

Treated and Dyed

Printed in Great Britain
by Amazon

21337401R00142